Tilda The Mail Order Bride

Sarah Amberson

Published by Trellis Publishing, 2021.

TILDA THE MAIL ORDER BRIDE

First edition. July 9, 2021.

Copyright © 2021 Sarah Amberson.

ISBN: 979-8223991106

Written by Sarah Amberson.

TILDA THE MAIL ORDER BRIDE

SARAH AMBERSON

—-*—-

"I'm sorry, there was nothing I could do." The doctor's somber voice barely reached Tilda's ears. Her little seven-year-old heart couldn't believe what was happening. She had gone from being a happy and normal child with two loving parents to an orphan with no one to turn to.

Tears didn't come right away, but once Tilda was alone, they began to flow down her cheeks in a steady stream.

It was only two days later that Tilda stood at the foot of her parents' coffins. The cholera epidemic had been merciless in their town. She didn't recognize many of the people who attended the funeral, but she was told they were from her parents' church. Many of them came to tell her how sorry they were her parents had passed away, but no one offered to take her home.

Even though Tilda was young, she had heard of the orphanages and already knew she didn't want to go there. Her parents had told her about the work they made the children do. She'd heard about how the children almost never found a family or a home and lived at the orphanage their whole lives.

"I'm sorry little one," the kind pastor said to her after most everyone had left. "I'll be taking you home for the night and tomorrow we'll have to be going to the orphanage," he explained patiently to her.

Tilda nodded. She knew there was nothing she could do about it. Her life was now in the control of others.

Tilda hardly slept during the night at the minister's house. The bed was strange and hard and there were strange noises in the room. The ceiling creaked and when the wind blew the branches of a tree outside the window tapped repeatedly on the glass. When she would drift off to sleep she would awake when she thought she heard her mother's or father's voice and instead saw that the nightmare was true, and she was still all alone.

The next morning the minister's wife gave her a small chunk of bread and some cheese wrapped up in a cloth and patted her on the head sympathetically. Soon Tilda was on the minister's wagon, heading towards the orphanage.

The large house building loomed large before her. It was a grey color and looked like something you might see in your nightmares. Vines grew up the sides of the large building, adding to the mysteriousness of the building. Giant pine trees touched the sides of the building which seemed to be several floors high. The dark windows looked down at her and her imagination supplied frightening specters watching her. Tilda clutched the minister's hand, so she wouldn't be so afraid. How could this be her new home?

As they pulled up the front, Tilda realized she didn't see any children. Maybe they were out working, or playing, or in school. The minister helped her down from the wagon and led her towards the large steps of the orphanage. She desired to break free and run away but the minister's hand held hers in a large iron grip and compelled her to follow

When they rang the bell, Tilda waited anxiously, wondering who would answer. She hoped there would be a nice lady who would care for her and teach her what to do. But the woman who opened the door was tall and stern looking with a long, pointed nose and dark eyes that seemed to look right through her. She appeared to be taller than anyone Tilda had ever seen before. She wore a long black dress that made a rustling sound when she moved.

Tilda shivered and took a step backward. The minister pulled her forward again and smiled down at her.

"It's alright. You will be fine," he reassured.

"Come in. This must be our new arrival," the lady said, her voice as cold as ice. She looked at Tilda as if she were about to buy an overpriced broken table.

"Yes, this is the orphan. Her name is Tilda," the minister said with a nervous chuckle. The woman did not smile or seem to find anything humorous about their arrival.

"Thank you. You may leave now," she announced.

"Goodbye, Tilda," the minister said, as he released her hand, passing her on to the headmistress. The woman pulled her into the building and closed the door abruptly behind Tilda.

She turned and led the way into the vast building. Tilda wanted to run back to the door, but she followed obediently.

As they walked through the bleak halls, Tilda's heart sank. Her life ahead looked as if it would be a very dreary one. The vaulted ceilings made her feel very small and afraid. Some of the windows in the great room had been boarded over and it was dark and hot. There were long rows of old wooden tables running through the room with benches of differing heights next to them.

The woman led her to the end of the hall and up a flight of narrow stairs to a room filled with rows of beds. All the beds were the same and they only had a foot of space between them. She led Tilda to one of the nondescript beds and wrote her name on a small placard hanging from the footboard.

"This will be your bed. You will keep your bed made properly at all times. You will get up at five in the morning and go to bed at eight in the evening. There will be no talking after curfew. There will be no exception to these rules. Do you understand?" the woman asserted firmly.

Tilda nodded but said nothing.

The woman stepped very close to her and spoke in a loud voice. "You will answer me when you are spoken to. Do you understand, child?"

"Yes, Ma'am," Tilda responded, close to tears.

"There will be no crying, shouting, or fighting in this house," the woman continued. "And you will study and work. Classes are in the morning, and in the afternoon, you will work in the sewing shop with the other girls. Do you understand?"

"Yes, Ma'am," Tilda responded again, trying to keep her emotions together.

"Alright. Follow me," the woman said, as she walked down the stairs and through several corridors to a large room filled with tables and chairs. There were several grim looking girls around the same age as Tilda. They looked up from their work but said nothing, and their eyes reflected fear when they looked at the headmistress.

"You will sit here," she announced. Mary, you teach her how to sew the buttons on shirts. Make sure she does it correctly or you will both be punished. Do you understand?"

Tilda climbed onto the chair and looked at the mountains of clothing on all of the tables. It seemed there was an endless supply of shirts. She sighed and took the needle the wide-eyed girl held out to her. She had no idea how endless the supply was.

—-*—-

Tilda held her chin high. She didn't know what to expect from her husband-to-be and felt butterflies in her stomach. She had never had the chance to court or fall in love at the orphanage, so the whole idea of marriage was a foreign one, but it was something she hadn't exactly had a choice in.

When she'd seen the ad for a mail-order bride, she knew that it was the only way she would get away from the orphanage without compromising herself.

Tilda shook her head, she didn't want to think about the orphanage, but it always seemed to find a way to weasel its way into her thoughts. The road they'd been traveling on was bumpy and uneven but surprisingly she had enjoyed the trip immensely. The sight out the window was absolutely beautiful after being in the city for most of her life and Tilda couldn't get enough of it.

Suddenly, a large ranch house came into view in the distance. It was the biggest house out in the west Tilda had seen so far. It appeared as if it had at least ten rooms and she was sure it had a huge parlor and kitchen and every other area one could imagine in a house. It was painted white with light blue trim around its windows and doors. The second story had large windows with blue shutters.

The green grass of the lawn looked well-tended. Trees, bushes and flowers framed the house with their colorful beauty. All in all it looked like a picture out of one of the fairy tales Tilda had heard when she was young.

She could see a trail leading away behind the house to a garden and barn. A paddock of horses grazed at the side of the barn. Another shed held the wagons and equipment. The garden appeared to be growing well and well cared for.

As they pulled up to the house, Tilda felt very uncertain. What if Hunter didn't like her? He had seemed rather cold in his letters and Tilda was never sure quite what to think.

As they pulled up to the large house, the wagon driver motioned for Tilda to go ahead and not worry about her things. Tilda nervously walked up to the door. It loomed above her, almost daring her to enter. Tilda timidly knocked on the white wood. When no one answered she knocked a little harder. A woman, who appeared to be a little older than herself, answered after several long minutes.

She reminded Tilda of the headmistress at the orphanage with her black hair pulled back into a bun, pointed nose, and cold look.

"Yes?" She stared down at Tilda in a superior way. Tilly could tell by her black dress and the white lace around her collar that she was the maid of the house. Tilda had never been to a house where they needed their own maid, but she had heard of them.

"I'm Tilda. I- I am Hunter's bride-to-be," Tilda said uncertainly. She wasn't exactly sure how to introduce herself in this situation. She felt very awkward and small, as she had when she first went to the orphanage.

The woman stared at her for a few uncomfortable moments before opening the door a little wider.

"Come in," the woman said flatly. "Hunter is waiting for you this way." As Tilda followed her down the halls she couldn't help but admire the fine woodwork. Whoever owned this house was very wealthy. Tilda wondered if it was her husband-to-be or someone else.

The woman led Tilda to the study and opened the door without knocking. "The woman is here," the maid announced in a slightly annoyed voice. "I will go for some tea." Her duty done, she turned and left without looking at Tilda, causing her to feel even more discomfort than before.

As they entered the study a man, presumably Hunter stood and came forward to meet her. His hair was dark and his eyes blue, giving him a striking countenance. He smiled politely and courteously took her hand but seemed rather business like and not overly friendly. He bowed slightly and offered Tilda a chair. She sat down but didn't know what to say.

"Well, I trust you had a pleasant voyage," he said, rather formally.

"Yes. It was so lovely! The flowers, the fields and trees! I haven't seen such beauty in years," she gushed with enthusiasm. I lived in the city ever since I was seven and they never allowed us to go out of the courtyard. She looked down, her enthusiasm suddenly dampened with the memory of the dismal years at the orphanage.

"Hmm that's too bad that you were always in the city. I had hoped that you would know how to work, he said, looking disappointed. He turned to the window. There is a good deal of work involved in being a wife and taking care of a place such as this one, he continued. You do understand that I will expect you to keep this house in proper order at all times. Maddie will teach you what needs to be done and will assist you. Am I clear?" he finished.

He turned back toward her and looked at her expectantly. She thought about the hundreds of times she had said "Yes ma'am" and now it would be "Yes sir." Well it had to be better than the orphanage. Now that she was an adult she would be able to do much more than sew buttons on shirts and hem skirts. And maybe in time he would even come to care for her if she was careful to do her part.

"Yes, sir, I understand," she replied, trying to maintain eye contact even though she felt intimidated. "I grew up in an orphanage and there we were taught to work. I hope I will please you.

"Good, good, then let's go into town and go before the justice and make this legal, he said in a cheerful tone of voice, offering her his arm. "We should be back in time for dinner."

—-*—-

Hunter felt a wave of exhaustion wash over him. He had been out hunting most the day. Normally he would be supervising workers on the ranch, or in town at the barber shop, but he'd needed some time to think.

Getting married out of the blue the day before had been a strange experience. He'd known from the moment he'd written to Tilda that he didn't want a wife for a relationship, or a family. What he really needed was to look proper in the towns eyes and it didn't hurt that a wife was responsible for household affairs.

He dismounted his horse and let the stable boy lead her away. He had already informed the maid that she would be taking orders from Tilda instead of from him, which of course she hadn't taken well. But she would just have to learn her place. After all she was just the maid.

Hunter headed towards the garden. He loved the garden and made sure the gardener had spent extra time planting roses and other flowering plants. He liked having somewhere he could sit and think when he came back from a stressful day. The garden was a perfect place for that.

As he entered the garden he checked on a couple of plants just to make sure they were watered and growing nicely. Even though the gardener did most of the work, Hunter always kept an eye on things to make sure they were being cared for properly.

Suddenly, he noticed that someone was crying. Hunter stopped. He wondered who it was. None of the ranch workers spent time in the garden and it caught him off guard that he wasn't alone. The other thing that caught him off guard was the crying. He hated it when women cried, he just didn't know what to do or what to say.

For a second, he thought about fleeing the garden and leaving whoever it was to their plight, but something made him move forward. There, under the large apple tree, sat his new wife. She wore a pale blue dress that stood out in the moonlight and was sitting on the small wooden bench he normally occupied at this time of night. Her head was in her hands and her shoulders were shaking delicately with light sobs.

Hunter watched for a second and he felt a pang of pity. What about her stay had been so awful that it had sent her out here to the garden to cry?

"Aggm," Hunter cleared his throat causing Tilda to look around, startled that she had been discovered.

"Oh, Hunter, I'm sorry. I-" she stammered nervously, wiping lingering tears from her cheeks.

"Whatever has you so upset?" The distrust that shown in Tilda's eyes made Hunter feel bad for being a little gruffer than he had intended.

"It's nothing. I should be getting back inside, I didn't mean to trouble you," she mumbled, hurrying to her feet and taking a couple steps towards away. She looked awkwardly at him.

"There must have been something to have caused such distress," Hunter insisted. At first, he hadn't really cared, but he suddenly wanted to know why his wife had been crying. He may not have had feelings for her yet, but he didn't want her to be hurt in his household.

"Just something was said, and I shouldn't have been listening." Tilda looked at him with uncertain eyes and Hunter saw in her eyes that this wasn't her first negative experience.

"Who said what?" Hunter demanded.

She looked at him fearfully. "I'm sorry, I didn't mean to cause any problem. I just... this wasn't what I was expecting, that's all." Tilda's vulnerable look disappeared, and a well-practiced mask fell over her features.

"I have said too much. Goodnight," she mumbled as she slipped past him before Hunter could say anything.

After she left, Hunter found himself more and more disturbed by her distress. She obviously hadn't felt she could tell him what had happened. The typical tranquility the garden brought him was shattered as it was now haunted by Tilda's crying figure sitting on the bench in Hunter's mind.

—-*—-

Tilda rose at her normal time and went straight to work. She'd been married to Hunter for nearly a week and had now established a sort of routine. Hunter was usually gone by the time she woke up in the morning and he came in late after she'd gone to bed. They hadn't seen each other much since the night in the garden. Hunter's interest in who had caused her distress had surprised Tilda. She hadn't expected him to care.

She had since formulated a plan to try and do everything she could for Hunter. Maybe, if she put forth efforts to do things that pleased him, he might even begin to care for her as he would for a wife of his own choosing. Tilda had wanted nothing more than a real family since she had been thrown into the orphanage life.

Her parents were still vaguely in her memory and their kind of relationship was what she hoped to find with Hunter. Now that she was here she didn't exactly have many options. It seemed as if Hunter was her one chance at having a family and for some reason he didn't seem to be very interested.

Tilda made her way to the kitchen. She had found out from the grocer in town that Hunter's favorite meal was a good chicken soup. Luckily for Tilda, she was an expert at cooking. The day outside was rainy and a little chilly so it was a perfect time to make hot chicken soup.

The grocer was apparently a good friend of Hunter's and Hunter had informed him that chicken soup reminded him of his mother's cooking and the life he used to have with his family. Maybe they had some things in common after all.

"Maddie, are you here?" Tilda called through the kitchen. Maddie appeared from behind a counter. The woman seemed to always be lurking and pop up in her path from the oddest places.

"What do you need now?" Maddie said with a condescending tone.

"I need you to run to town and pick these things up for me." Tilda said, holding out a small piece of paper with a list of the things she would need.

Maddie read over the items and scowled at Tilda, "Spending his money already, are you?" She said with a harsh chuckle before walking off. Tilda stood in the middle of the floor feeling dumbfounded. She didn't know what to say to the woman. It wasn't as if she were buying anything for herself. Not quite sure whether Maddie would actually go and get the things as requested, Tilda hoped for the best and went to talk to Lee.

Lee was the kindest worker in Hunter's household. He was an older man, most likely in his sixties and had been the household cook for a number of years. He had a reputation for being able to cook anything up. He had been friendly to Tilda despite the rest of the staff's feelings.

"Lee, I'd like to help make Hunter something special for dinner," she said as she approached.

Lee looked up with a gleam in his eye. "The way to a man's heart is through his stomach," Lee exclaimed with a hearty laugh. "You are one smart little lady." Tilda had no choice but to join in with Lee's laugh. It was contagious in a good kind of way.

Surprisingly, when Tilda came back to the kitchen a couple of hours later, she found the supplies she had requested on the table and Lee had already begun chopping the carrots. She put her apron on and together they made chicken soup, and she found herself thinking how it would be to be working alongside her parents if they wouldn't have passed away so many years ago. She felt bad for all the years she had missed, but she found herself enjoying working alongside Lee as he told her stories about Hunter and his ranching experiences.

When Hunter came home he was pleased that she had made him his favorite meal, and she glowed as she sat across from him. He seemed relaxed and conversational and they stayed at the table long after the dishes had been taken away, talking and sharing stories of their past. The time passed quickly and both of them were surprised when they noticed that the rest of the household had retired to their beds.

—-*—-

Hunter awoke and turned over in the big four post bed to face his new bride. He looked for several minutes at her sleeping face, noticing the long, curved eyelashes and rosy cheeks. She really was a beautiful young woman. There was something sad about her face, as if she had never learned to be happy.

He thought back to the night before. She had seemed happy then, bringing his favorite meal to him and serving it as if he had won a prize. And the soup had been truly wonderful. Lee was a good cook, but he had to admit her soup had even surpassed Lee's talents. They had talked and laughed together so easily. It had surprised him that she had been so easy to talk to. The hours had slipped by quickly.

He found himself appreciating her at every turn. Maddie was angry and sullen that she had to take orders from his new bride, but Tilda had not complained. She seemed to rise above the pettiness and look the other way. She didn't shy away from giving orders, but she wasn't haughty about it either. She seemed to have gained much wisdom during her years of suffering at the hands of the orphanage headmistress. He certainly had to admire her for that.

He suddenly remembered that his brother was coming for a visit and cut his ruminations short. He had to get up and get some work done quickly. He got out of bed and dressed quietly. He would let her sleep in a little. They had stayed up so late the night before.

—-*—-

Tilda woke up to find the sun was already high in the sky. She sat up quickly, Hunter was already gone. She wondered why he hadn't wakened her. The maid had informed her the day before that Hunter's brother was going to come for a visit. She wanted everything to be perfect. After all, what his family thought of her was important. She dressed quickly, feeling ashamed that she had slept so late.

She checked the guest bedroom and had Maddie check that everything was prepared. Finally, she felt that everything was ready, and she waited anxiously for his arrival. She wondered what sort of man he would be and if he approved of his brother getting a bride by mail.

When he rode up on his horse with Hunter outside, Tilda could see the resemblance. They looked almost like twins. She had heard his brother was only two years older than Hunter.

Hunter handed off their horses the stable hand and they made their way inside.

"Hello there. Hunter, this must be your new wife?" Hunter's brother motioned towards Tilda in a questioning manner.

"Sure is," Hunter said. He seemed a little uncomfortable and rocked back and forth on his feet.

"Nice to meet you missus," the man said kindly with a drawl.

"Come, let me show you to your room," Hunter said, drawing his brother's attention away from Tilda.

After they had gone, Tilda wondered why Hunter had been in such a hurry. She hoped she hadn't done something to disappoint him.

Hurrying towards the kitchen she went to see if everything was set for dinner. Fried chicken and mashed potatoes with peach cobbler and tea was what had been planned to be prepared and Tilda wanted to make sure everything was perfect.

"Is Hunter's brother here yet?" a very busy Lee asked.

"Yes, he just arrived," Tilda said quickly. "Is everything ready?"

Cook looked at her like she'd asked a ridiculous question.

"Of course, everything's ready. When have I not had things ready?" Tilda laughed. Cook was right, he did usually have things ready and perfectly too.

"Okay," Tilda laughed. "I'll call them for dinner. It smells delicious!"

She hurried from the kitchen up the stairs to the bedroom Hunter's brother would be staying in. As she neared the top of the stairs, she heard voices wafting down the hall to the stairs. She paused, and although she knew eavesdropping was not a mannerly practice, she couldn't seem to move her feet forward.

"So, what's it like being married?" It was most definitely Hunter's brother asking the question.

"It's fine. You know, I didn't really want a wife. I just wanted all the women in town to stop chasing me down, but it's not bad having someone to take care of stuff around the house." Hunter and his brother laughed together.

Tilda took the last three steps and turned down the hall the other direction to her room. She couldn't stand to hear anymore. She nearly collided with Maddie on her way to her room.

"Maddie, please inform Hunter and his brother that dinner is ready. I'm not feeling well and will take mine in my room." Tilda didn't wait for Maddie to respond but continued quickly on to the bedroom that was now her only escape, even if for only a few hours.

—-*—-

The ride back to the house with his brother, John had been exhilarating. The warm afternoon and sunshine was welcome after the previous three days of rain and cold. They raced the horses across the field and John got to the yard two lengths ahead of him. They laughed together as they dismounted. They had always seemed to be in a competition with each other since they were small boys.

He felt uneasy about introducing his brother to his wife. He knew that his brother had had a very bad experience with marriage, and he didn't want to hear him tell him again what a bad idea marriage was.

As they came in, Tilda seemed to be waiting in the parlor. His brother seemed to take great interest in her and he suddenly felt jealously protective of her, to his surprise. Hunter steered his brother to the stairs, anxious to show him to his room and make sure he had everything he needed.

"So, what's it like being married?" his brother asked, a mischievous gleam in his eye.

Hunter knew that his brother's experience with marriage had been a bad one. He had come into some rough luck with the woman, who had treated him terribly and made off with most of his money. He really wished he didn't have to talk about it with John.

"It's fine. You know, I didn't really want a wife. I just wanted all the women in town to stop chasing me down, but it's not bad having someone to take care of stuff around the house." Hunter joined in with his brother laughing. He paused for a moment.

"But you know," he continued thoughtfully, "she really turned out to be something. She's organized everything like never before and is quite intelligent. I do believe I've begun to fall in love with her," Hunter finished on a serious note.

"Well, do be careful brother, but she does look like a real nice girl, so you might have gotten lucky." Hunter's brother gave him a hearty slap on the back. Hunter was surprised that John didn't have anything negative to say at all. He felt relieved.

"Come on, let's go see if my wife has some supper on the table for us." Hunter led the way towards the kitchen. It sure did smell good.

—-*—--

Tilda lay on her bed. She wanted to cry but she just felt empty inside. The tears wouldn't come. She decided that if all Hunter wanted was a maid then a maid she would be. He had seemed embarrassed to even introduce her to his brother. He hadn't even given her a chance to answer him.

And then he had said to his brother that he didn't even want her. Why had he ordered her if he didn't want her? She was just to show the town that he had a wife?

She wondered if she had done something wrong. She had tried to do special things for him, but he still didn't seem to want her. She thought of the night before when they had laughed together after supper. He had seemed happy. She really didn't understand. Maybe this was the way men were.

Well, she would do the work that she knew he expected of her and just leave him alone. If he was interested in her he would have to come and find her. Maybe it would take much longer for him to realize her value. She would just have to be patient and accept whatever fate came her way.

—-*—-

Hunter and John went down to the kitchen with hungry anticipation. The smell of fresh bread filled the house and made Hunter's mouth water. He was amazed at the meals they had eaten since Tilda had come to be with him. Lee had always been a good cook, but Tilda seemed to relish in small details like fresh bread or muffins and always served the meal with a childlike joy.

Hunter was surprised that Tilda was no where to be seen and Maddie was serving the meal in her usual dour manner.

"Where is Tilda?" he asked.

"Your wife informed me that she wouldn't be coming to dinner. She said she wasn't feeling well and would be in her room." She looked as if she wished to say more but changed her mind. She sniffed and busied herself in the kitchen.

In the days that followed Hunter saw very little of Tilda. It seemed that when he came home from work she was always busy in some other part of the house. She still cooked special breads and meals but no longer served them. He felt annoyed at Maddie's patronizing attitude and missed the sunny demeanor of his new wife.

One afternoon he stood in the parlor and looked out into the garden and saw her sitting on the bench under the apple tree, looking forlorn. She bent over and smelled the roses one by one and he could see that she was crying. What had he done to make her so unhappy? He suddenly realized how much he missed her. Without realizing it he had begun to love her.

—-*—-

Tilda walked through the garden admiring the flowers as the sun lowered in the sky towards evening. It had been a beautiful day. The sun had been warm and pleasant. She had finished cleaning all of the upstairs rooms and making bread and although the day had been pleasant enough she felt very lonely.

It wasn't that she was unthankful. For the most part no one bothered her, and she was free to do as she pleased as long as she kept the household running smoothly. It was a lot of work, but it was good work and she would never have to be humiliated by the headmistress from the orphanage again, and if she sewed a button on a shirt it was because one had fallen off and needed replacement.

She enjoyed the garden tremendously, never tiring of the roses and other flowers and their sweet scents and delicate colors. She also enjoyed feeding the chickens and gathering their eggs. They were often comical creatures and ran to her crazily whenever she came to their pen with scraps from the kitchen. She had secretly named several of them but felt too silly to share that information with anyone.

But still she felt alone and disappointed that Hunter never sought her out. She had secretly hoped that he would come to her, but he hadn't. Today it seemed too much to bear, and she cried silently as she smelled the sweet roses one by one.

She heard a sound behind her and turned around to find Hunter there standing next to the tree. She had not heard him approach, being distracted with her feelings of woe. She stood speechless, her cheeks red with embarrassment at being caught crying in the garden once again.

He cleared his throat and looked at her sympathetically. "I usually come to the garden to think and you come here to cry. The flowers are good listeners," he added quietly.

"I'm sorry. I should be more thankful," she responded. "I don't know what comes over me sometimes. I guess I just feel alone.

"I know. That's my fault and I am so sorry. When I first wrote to you I thought I wanted a wife just to take care of the house and so that I was a respectable man in the eyes of the people. But since you came here I have learned that there is much more that comes with marriage." He looked very somber.

"You brought joy and sunshine into my life when you came. And these last two weeks without you have been gray and rainy weeks. I want my sunshine back. I miss you," he finished.

Tilda didn't know what to say. She felt like a flower blossoming under the sun. His words had sent the clouds away like a vapor and she felt her joy return.

He reached out for her hands and pulled her into his embrace. "Will you *really* be my wife?" he asked, with thick emotion in his voice. She looked up into his eyes and smiled.

"I will," she responded, and she felt happier than she ever had before.

Epilogue

Tilda stared out the open window at all the activity below. It was a chilly day and she was avoiding the cold, otherwise she'd be right outside with everyone else.

They had invited family and friends for a dinner party to celebrate their big news. After three years they had finally found that they were expecting a new addition to their family. Tilda was happier than any young woman could ever be.

She had never expected the happiness she had found with Hunter and now they would be starting a family of their own. Tilda already imagined what it would be like to have their little son or daughter playing in the halls of the house or sitting by the fire, listening to one of Hunter's delightful stories.

The years had progressed nicely, and it felt like a hundred years had passed since Tilda had come to be a mail-order bride for Hunter. She smiled at the memories. There had been so many misunderstandings and frustrations along the way, but in the end, they had come to love each other, and Tilda didn't know what she would do without Hunter.

"How are you, my dear?" Hunter's kind voice interrupted her thoughts. He gave her a long hug and a little kiss on her cheek.

"How is our little one?" Hunter looked expectantly at Tilda's stomach.

"We are both doing fine," Tilda reassured him with a smile, as she set another plate of steaming food on the table.

"Can you call everyone to eat?" she requested.

As their guests filed in, Tilda greeted each one with eagerness. Soon they were all seated at the table, heaping their plates full and sharing stories about the last couple months of their lives.

Tilda smiled at Hunter. She had finally found the family she had dreamed of so long ago, and it was perfect.

Amish Innocence

26

MONICA MARKS

Lavina gasped and whirled, startled at the door slammed against the barn wall. Her hand flew to her throat as if to steady her heartrate.

"Lizzie!" she breathed at her sister. "You must be more careful with the door!"

Elizabeth Blauch grinned sheepishly and looked at the swinging wood.

"Sorry, Lavvy. I always forget how temperamental it can be."

She smiled at the abashed girl as her pulse regained normalcy.

"It has been this way for as long as we have been on this earth," she replied, laughing.

"More the reason I would always imagined it would have been fixed by now!" Elizabeth retorted.

Lavina stepped out of the stable, placing the broom against the door. She dusted off her hands on a simple white apron before returning her attention to her sister.

"Are you looking for me?" she asked, securing the empty stall and Lizzie looked uncomfortable.

"Yes..."

Lavina waited, staring expectantly at Elizabeth to finish but the girl seemed unwilling to speak.

"Are we playing a guessing game, Lizzie?"

"I wanted to tell you that Eli came calling," Elizabeth blurted out.

She whirled to face her sister, her brown eyes narrowing in annoyance.

"What could he possibly want this time?" she growled and Elizabeth sighed.

"He left a note," she replied, handing a folded piece of paper to her. The older sister shook her auburn head and scowled at the message.

"Use it in the wood stove," she snapped. "He has nothing to say that I want to hear."

Lizzie nodded in agreement, ripping the letter in two pieces.

"You are so strong, Lavina. Another woman would have fallen to pieces after what he did to you."

Lavina did not respond and the two walked from the barn where the older sister had spent the afternoon cleaning.

She did not hear me sobbing into my pillow at night afterward, she thought, glancing at Lizzie out of her peripheral vision. Lizzie skipped along lightly and Lavina was overcome by a fusion of affection and shame.

She adored her sisters. Lizzie was the second youngest and Lavina the second oldest. They were very close both in age and in spirit and Lavina shared most of her thoughts with the high spirited younger girl.

Most of them. If she knew everything, she would be so hurt.

Lizzie's abrupt appearance in the stables had shocked her but not because of the unruly barn door. Lavina had been lost in thought, thoughts she had no business thinking.

Guilt and consternation had swept through her as she stared at her sister as if Lizzie was able to see what she was planning.

What am I planning? Lavina asked herself grouchily. *You have yet to figure that out for yourself.*

"Lavvy, have you heard a word I spoke?"

More humiliation flooded through the older sibling and her pale skin turned crimson. Lizzie immediately saw the heat in her cheeks.

"Why are you blushing?"

Lavina turned her head as they approached the house.

"It is hot today," she fibbed, the words leaving a strange taste in her mouth. She was unaccustomed to lying, especially to her family. Lizzie continued to stare at her.

"It is not that hot," Lizzie muttered, opening the side door to allow Lavina inside but the lovely redhaired girl shook her head.

"No, I have work to do in the garden yet," she told her sister. Lizzie threw her hands up in exasperation, her own coffee colored eyes darkening with suspicion.

"Lavina, are you certain you are alright?"

The older sister nodded quickly, offering her sister a tight smile.

"Yes, of course."

"It is almost time for supper. The garden can wait until tomorrow," Lavina told her. As she opened her mouth to argue, Elizabeth spoke again.

"I suspect that Eli might return."

Lavina gritted her teeth.

"He will not if he knows what is good for him," she grumbled but she glanced at Lizzie's concerned face and relented.

"Yes, you are right," she agreed, sighing. She did wish to be caught alone with Eli that afternoon or any other for that matter. It was bad enough she was forced to see him in the community and at worship.

He should not be coming around. I will have Daed talk to his father or the deacon. This is becoming harassment.

Lavina did not wish to go that route for it would arouse a lot of questions she did not wish to answer and shine a negative light on Eli. It went against the bronze haired beauty's gentle way to create ripples. She hoped that her ex-boyfriend's fixation on her would falter but she suspected that he was only getting started.

It is not me whom he wants; he is simply angered that I caught onto his sneaky, despicable ways and he could not talk his way out of them. He thinks he can woo me back with his charm but I am wise to who he is now. I will never go back, no matter how many letters he leaves or flowers he sends.

In a way, Lavina was grateful having discovered Eli's girlfriend in a neighboring district. She had no idea how he thought he would have gotten away with such a cunning deception but he had managed throughout their entire six-month courtship while Lavina patiently waited for a marriage proposal.

It was not until the other woman had grown distrustful of Eli's comings and goings that she surprised him at worship one Sunday morning and Eli had found himself caught.

To the girl's credit, she had not caused a scene, quietly wishing him and Lavina good luck before retreating in her wagon to her own district. Lavina had then been faced with a difficult choice; forgiveness or turn her back on the man she had been certain she was going to marry.

"If he could do such a brazenly disrespectful thing to you for half a year, Lavvy, he is hardly the wagon which you would want to hitch your horse to," Lizzie had told her and Lavina knew her sister was right.

It was at that time that Lavina began to question her desire to stay in the Amish community.

The Ordnung is meant to keep us humble and free of the influences and desires which outsiders enshroud themselves, Lavina thought sadly. *But there is no more security here than there is beyond here. We are secluded to be protected and together but we can be just as alienated and alone as anywhere else.*

Lavina had been baptized the year before, her faith unwavering before the blow she had been delivered by Eli's infidelity. She had never wanted a life beyond the sanctuary of the one she had known in Holmes County. Yet almost overnight, something had changed within her. Eli had created a distrust in her and a yearning to escape. While she had not spoken of Eli's cruelty to anyone, she could not shake the sense that people were talking about her. Lavina felt eyes on her everywhere she went.

She had decided that she would not stand for it any longer.

"Lavina, you are beginning to concern me," Lizzie told her quietly and she realized she had once more drifted off in thought.

"I apologize," she told her sister. "I was just pondering why that man will not leave well enough alone."

"You should go directly to his parents and tell them what kind of boy they have raised," Lizzie announced as they washed their hands. Rebecca looked up from the island in the kitchen where she was chopping vegetables.

"Are you speaking of Eli?" she asked and Lizzie nodded. The middle sister sighed inwardly. She was truly not in the mood to discuss her ex.

"What he did is reproachful. Someone should put him in his proper place. Lavvy, have you spoken with the deacon about this atrocity?"

"No, she has not spoken to anyone!" Lizzie sighed with annoyance.

"And I wish you would stop speaking of it also," Lavina snapped. Her sisters stared at her in surprise. The gentle redhead did not often raise her voice.

"We are concerned for you," Rebecca told her, turning back to the task on the counter but Lavina could read the hurt in her expression.

"I know you are but I would much rather forget the entire sordid affair," she said softly, wishing to strike the stricken look from her sister's face.

An awkward silence ensued.

"What else needs to be done?" Lavina asked Rebecca, indicating the dinner preparation but she shook her dark hair.

"Nothing. We are having a visitor for supper," she said in a clipped tone and Lavina knew that Rebecca wanted to brood alone. Rebecca was the least forgiving of the four siblings, apt to long bouts of sulking when her feelings were hurt.

"Who is coming?" Lizzie asked. Rebecca's brown eyes flashed.

"I do not know! An outsider."

Elizabeth and Lavina stared at one another in surprise but they knew pushing Rebecca for more information would be futile. Her mood was already ruined.

"I will be in my room," Lavina announced and her younger sister tried to follow her but she stopped Lizzie at the threshold.

"I would like to lay down for a moment before supper," she told her sister. An expression of hurt crossed over Lizzie's face but she nodded begrudgingly.

"Are you feeling unwell?"

"My head is hurting," Lavina answered truthfully. "I may have been in the sun too long without water today."

"Shall I get you something to drink?"

Shame sparked through the older sister again.

You have a family who loves you dearly. How can you be considering such an atrocious act? You will disrupt their lives with your own selfishness.

"Yes, that would be lovely, Lizzie."

Elizabeth's rosebud mouth curved into a happy smile and she turned to run back down the stairs, eager to help.

Quickly, Lavina slipped into her room and dropped to her knees at her bed. Glancing furtively at the closed door, she dug around under the mattress, her hand closing around a piece of paper at the center of the twin bed and pulled it out.

She had read it many times in the past month but it did not deter her from scanning it again.

This is the paper which will give me options in the English world. Without it, I will not stand a chance.

She heard her sister climbing the wood stairs and Lavina carefully replaced the document back in its hiding spot, jumping onto the bed. A second later, Elizabeth entered with a glass of water.

"You will never guess who *Daed* invited to supper," her younger sister gushed, thrusting the water to Lavina in excitement. She redhead accepted it and took a dutiful sip, trying to seem interested. Obviously, Elizabeth had pressed Rebecca for more details when she went downstairs.

"Who?" she asked.

"An Englisher!"

Lavina felt her heart speed up. It was not unusual for their father to invite outsiders for supper. Not only was Elmo Blauch a skilled furniture maker in the community doing business with the English daily, he was also a minister. People from all walks of life found themselves in their humble dining room breaking bread.

Yet that day, the word "Englisher" sent a fission of alarm coursing through Lavina as if whomever was coming was about to decide which course which she was going to embark upon.

"Why is this news?" Lavina asked nonchalantly, averting her dark eyes toward the bed nervously.

"He is trying to become Amish!" Lizzie declared gleefully. Lavina's eyes jumped to her sister's face to gage if she was joking.

"*He is trying to become Amish?*" she echoed. "I did not realize the church allowed for such things to happen."

Elizabeth shrugged.

"I did not either but according to Rebecca, this man has been in the district for one week already."

"Where is he staying?" Suddenly Lavina was fascinated.

I wonder what would instill such a sudden desire in someone. Has he no family? No one he will miss if he adopts our way of life?

"He has been living with Mary and Jacob Umble."

"How unusual," Lavina mumbled and her sister nodded in agreement.

"I will leave you to rest but supper will be ready soon," she said, turning for the door. She paused to toss a smile back at Lavina.

"I would offer to bring yours here but I suspect you do not wish to miss this."

"No," Lavina conceded. "I will be there for certain."

She watched as Elizabeth closed the door to the bedroom she shared with Rebecca and listened for her light footsteps to continue out of earshot.

How interesting. Perhaps Gott is giving me a sign. He is sending someone here to take my place when I leave.

Again, Lavina's eyes shifted to the mattress and she thought of the paper under her frame.

I took a big risk obtaining my General Education Diploma without the knowledge of my family. I am fortunate I was not caught but without it, I will be unable to secure a future outside of the community. When the time is right, I will bid good bye to my family and move to the city to start a new life, away from the Amish and away from Eli Smucker.

When Ruby Plank had appeared at worship that fateful Sunday, quietly confronting Eli in her presence, Lavina had wanted to run away and hide forever. Her sisters had been told about his indiscretion and sworn to secrecy but Lavina could not shake the sense of feeling smothered by the community.

If I leave, I will never be welcomed back, not when I have already committed myself to Gott and the Ordnung. I must be sure I am well prepared to go and leave behind everyone.

Immediately, Lavina had enrolled in adult classes at the Holmes Community Center, determined to acquire her GED. She had secretly been fashioning English clothing to wear, slowly gathering a bag which she could take when the moment was right. It was filled with necessities like money, toiletries and snacks.

What else do you need? You are ready to go, she told herself. Lavina knew what she needed; assurance that she was doing the right thing.

As she trudged down the stairs to meet the family for supper, she wondered if she was simply growing cowardly.

You have had your GED for a month, sneaking about like a thief in the night to get it and now you are sitting on your hands as if you have lost your nerve. You must go. You can tell everyone tomorrow and leave on Friday morning. It is time. Eli will continue to be a constant reminder of his own betrayal and you will not feel peace until you are away from him.

"Lavina, are you going to join us or do you intend to eat from the doorway?" Her mother demanded, laughing and Lavina realized she had stopped in the doorway. She flashed her already seated family a brief smile which faded as she saw the stranger in their midst. She lowered her eyes and shuffled toward the table.

"I was laying down," she mumbled, taking her seat.

"If you are unwell, Lavvy, you may take your supper in your room," Belinda Blauch told her daughter but Lavina shook her head.

"No, *Mammi,* I am fine to have supper at the table."

She nodded at the man who sat wedged between her father and Rebecca.

"Adam Everly, this is our fourth daughter, Lavina. Lavina, Adam is new to the community," Elmo announced. Adam stared at her with solemn blue eyes and she felt her heart momentarily ceased to beat. It was not so much an electricity but an undercurrent of sadness she felt from him. It pulsated across the table and filled Lavina with a melancholy she had never felt.

Lavina smiled tightly.

"Welcome, Adam."

"Hannah, will you lead prayer please?" Elmo asked his youngest daughter. Hannah lowered her auburn head and the family followed suit but Lavina found herself eyeing the newcomer covertly.

He was pleasantly attractive with dark blonde hair and rugged features but Lavina could see a stress in his face, a gaunt tightness.

Hannah finished and the family reached for the generous meal placed about the table.

"Where do you hail from, Adam?" Elizabeth asked eagerly. She wasted no time tracking the truth about the man. Rebecca scowled but Lavina could see her listening for a response as she chewed.

"Toledo," Adam replied quickly. Hannah peered at him quizzically and then about the table.

"Oh, I misunderstood," she said, swallowing a forkful of vegetables. "I thought our father was saying you are living in the district."

She seemed confused and Lavina understood why; Adam was dressed as an Amish man. He wore a simple white shirt, suspenders and black, homespun pants.

Elmo cleared his throat and glanced furtively at his wife.

"Adam is looking to convert to our way of life," Elmo replied. Hannah's mouth dropped open in shock but she quickly regained her composure.

"Oh! Oh...well...welcome..." she trailed off lamely, looking to her sisters for assistance. Rebecca and Elizabeth stared at their plates but Lavina could not help herself from staring at the stranger who seemed just as uncomfortable as her youngest sister.

"How are you enjoying our way of life so far?" Lavina heard herself asking. "Surely you must be missing the city and its luxuries by now."

Adam met her gaze and Lavina read defiance but he seemed to relax as he understood she was genuinely asking him and not mocking his choice.

"No," he answered simply. "I do not miss anything about the city."

"Adam has given himself one month to learn our traditions and a basic comprehension of Pennsylvania German," Elmo told his family, smiling fondly at he man.

"That is a steep timeline, Adam," Belinda protested. "There is much to learn."

"I am able to do this," Adam assured her. "If I can find the proper instructors, I am certain I can meet this target date."

"May I ask why the rush?" Lavina heard herself question.

Why do you care? Lavina wished she had the good sense to stop speaking. *You have enough to worry about without getting involved with this outsider's business.*

A shadow crossed over Elmo's face and before Adam could respond he spoke.

"Adam is ambitious. That is a virtuous quality in a man," the minister replied.

"I thought patience was a virtue," Elizabeth chimed and Belinda gave her daughter a reproving look.

"I find his determination refreshing," Elmo told his family meaningfully. "And I wish to help his fulfill his quest. This is why I have enlisted Lavina to help him."

The family stared at him in shock, no one less so than his second born. When she regained her composure, she immediately protested.

"*Daed*, I have chores to attend – "

"There is nothing which demands your specific presence. Rebecca, Lizzie and Hannah can help where needed. Adam has already been in Holmes County for a week which means he is a week behind his goal already. You will teach him the ways of the Amish, Lavina."

Lavina found herself staring balefully at the newcomer who had the decency to appear shamed.

"*Dat*, surely a man would be a better teacher than me. Perhaps you can – "

"Lavina, if I had time, I would happily take Adam under my wing and guide him. Your mother and I are consumed with the store and I also have my duties as minister which to attend. Rebecca must oversee the farm. I am asking you to help a member of your community."

He is not a member of our community! He is an outsider who knows nothing of our ways and who is ruining my plans of leaving.

Everyone stared at Lavina, waiting for a response. She had no choice.

"Tomorrow morning, then, Adam?" she replied, trying to keep the acid from her voice. He nodded gratefully and the family exhaled collectively.

Three weeks is not a terribly long period. I will teach this man what I can and then I will tell my family I am leaving.

Lavina would not admit to herself that she was slightly relieved at the unexpected turn of events. She had not been looking forward to the backlash which her announcement would cause and her father had inadvertently afforded her more time.

It will give me a chance to choose the proper words and soften the hit with everyone, Lavina thought as she rode toward the Umble farm.

Approaching, she saw that Adam was already hard at work on the front porch, painting.

"You are early to rise," she commented, stepping down from the wagon. Adam rose from where he was painting the spindles and smiled briefly.

"I started this yesterday and tried to get it finished before going to your house but I didn't have a chance. I didn't want Mr. and Mrs. Umble to stare at a half-painted patio all day."

"Mary and Jacob," Lavina corrected. Adam stared at her uncomprehendingly.

"Pardon?"

"You should refer to them as Mary and Jacob. We do not use terms like mister and missus. We do not formalize."

Adam looked crushed by the lesson and Lavina smiled to take the seemingly harsh connotation from her words.

"It is different than your custom, I know but our way is one of simplicity. We do not overcomplicate our lives with titles."

"I have been calling them mister and missus for a week," he confessed. "And they did not say a word."

"They did not want to embarrass you but I am here to guide you in our ways and customs so forgive me if I do not hold back. It is not meant to undermine, only instruct."

Adam shook his head, his sky-blue eyes wide with gratitude.

"No, no thank you! I appreciate it!"

"Thank you is another term we use extremely sparingly."

Adam stared at her.

"You aren't serious."

"I am. We are perpetually in a state of thankfulness. It does not need to be expressed continuously."

"I am out of my element here," Adam muttered to himself and Lavina laughed.

"Think of this as moving to another country. You would need to learn the way of life anywhere you went if you wished to assimilate well. This is no different."

Adam nodded slowly.

"Well, now that we have conquered etiquette, where should we go?"

"I thought you might want a driving lesson. Have you handled a wagon before?"

Adam glanced at the cart and laughed.

"It looks pretty straightforward," he said and Lavina nodded seriously.

"Excellent. You may drive then."

The pair stepped toward the cart and Lavina watched as Adam struggled to climb onto the wagon. She smothered a smile.

This will be entertaining, she thought and she was not disappointed. As she climbed in beside him, she observed as he took the reins, pulling back too hard. The horse whinnied and turned to glare at him and Lavina could not help but laugh aloud. Adam cast her a sidelong look and hung his head.

"Okay, maybe it is not as straightforward as I initially thought," he said, handing her the straps.

"Do not lose faith. It will take a bit of practice. This is how you get her to move."

Lavina showed him how to urge the mare forward and without resistance, the horse started forward.

"You make it look so easy," he commented as they rode along. Lavina pointed out various family's farms, explaining their crafts while giving pointers for driving.

"I believe it is in my bloodline now," Lavina replied. She looked speculatively at Adam.

"Why have you decided to make such a drastic change in your life?"

Adam stared straight ahead without responding but Lavina saw a muscle twitch in his jawline.

"I apologize. I did not intend to upset you but I imagine I will not be the only person asking this question," she told him softly. "You need not answer me."

Adam seemed to relax but he did not look at her.

"Sometimes you just get a wake-up call and realize that everything you've ever known is not necessarily everything you've always needed. I don't know if that makes any sense to you."

It made perfect sense to Lavina and she almost laughed.

"What makes you believe that you will find the peace you are seeking here with us?"

Adam turned and faced her, an undecipherable expression on his face.

"I can't think of a time that I have felt more at peace than this minute," he replied and Lavina felt a slow blush rise into her cheeks.

They stopped outside of Millersburg and Lavina pointed to the quaint town.

"Our family's furniture shop is there," she told him. "I can show it to you another time."

"Why not now?" he asked and Lavina looked at him in surprise. She did not expect that he would be interested.

"Fine," she agreed and the continued on Railroad Street toward East Jackson Street. "May I ask what you did for a living in Toledo?"

"I was a financial advisor," he told her. Lavina found herself staring at him open-mouthed.

"Were you successful?"

"Very."

She stopped herself from asking any more questions despite her burning desire.

If he wants to tell me more, he will. But why would a rich man throw everything away to live so simply among the Amish? What does he see here that I do not?

"This is our family store," she told him as they pulled in front of the modest shop on North Grant Street. Adam leaned forward to peer into the store, his azure eyes shining with appreciation.

"Your people take so much pride in their work. There is such a sense of honor and family in your community. It is not like that with us."

Not all of them, Lavina thought sourly, thinking of Eli and his philandering ways. *There are unscrupulous people everywhere.*

Immediately, Lavina wondered what was wrong with her. She was in the company of a charming, appreciative man and her mind was wandering toward a serpent in the grass.

You should enjoy your time with this man while you are still here, she told herself.

They drove around town a while longer before heading back toward the district.

"Will I see you again tomorrow?" Adam asked hopefully and Lavina nodded.

"Tomorrow we will practice our Pennsylvania German. How much do you know?"

Adam gave her a look which told her she had much work to accomplish.

I will have to simply speak only to him in our language so he learns, Lavina decided.

Driving away from the Umble farm, Lavina found herself glancing over her shoulder to see if he was watching after her. He was.

The days began to pass at rapid speed and suddenly, two weeks had gone by. Adam had proven to be a model student and their time had begun to sway Lavina's thoughts of leaving.

Instead, she found herself more consumed with wanting to hold his hand and maybe steal a kiss.

Once he is baptized, he will be regarded as a member of this community just as anyone else. Perhaps we will have a future together, Lavina thought one evening, staring dreamily out the window as she did the supper dishes.

"Who is that Englisher you are always with?"

Lavina dropped the plate in her hand and whirled to confront the man who had crept into the kitchen. She glanced around but he family had retired to the front room and were out of earshot.

"Eli, do you not know how to use the front door?" she demanded, furiously. She bent down to pick up the broken dish at her feet.

"I asked you a question," he demanded, advancing on her. Lavina sprung to her feet and glared at him.

"You have no right to ask me anything. Get out of here before I call for my father, Eli!" she snapped but her heart was racing. His hazel eyes narrowed dangerously.

"You cannot walk out of my life that simply, Lavina. We are going to be married."

Lavina snorted and parted her lips to call for Elmo but to her relief, Eli stepped back and put his hand on the doorknob.

"You should really reconsider how you are treating me, Lavina."

He was gone before she could respond and Lavina sank against the sink, her heart pounding furiously in her chest.

Lavina raced to the top of the stairs where her sisters were already gathered.

"What is going on?" she hissed and they shushed her in unison. She crouched down to watch the scene at the front door where her father was speaking to another elder.

"...he refuses to repent. He is just sitting there smirking like a petulant child."

"I do not care about that right now," Elmo growled in a low tone, glancing back up at the stairwell. From his position, he could not see his daughters but he could likely sense them. When someone came knocking at three o'clock in the morning, it was apt to wake up the entire household.

"Where is the boy?"

The neighbor sighed and shook his head.

"He was taken by ambulance to Joel Pomerene Memorial Hospital. It was awful. So much blood..."

Elmo reached for his hat and coat, shaking his head.

"What happened?" Lavina demanded again. "Who got hurt."

Simultaneously, the three women turned to stare sympathetically at her.

"Lavina, Eli Smucker went to the Umble's home and beat Adam Everly with a wrought iron pipe," Elizabeth whispered.

Lavina screamed.

"*Daed,* go faster, please!" Lavina begged as they plodded toward the hospital in Millersburg.

"It does not matter how fast we go, Lavina. They will not allow for us to see him when we arrive," Elmo replied gently. The thought that she would not see Adam filled her with panic.

"Why not? Someone needs to be there for him!"

"If he is not in intensive care, we will see him when visiting hours start."

Intensive care? How badly did Eli hurt him? He is a madman! How can someone do something like that to another human being?

"Adam will never stay now," she breathed, the realization bringing about a sweeping bout of nausea.

"He will," Elmo assured her.

"How can you believe that? He came here because he thought people were different here. Now he will see that we have just as much evil and corruption as anywhere else."

"No Lavina, he came here because he was dying," Elmo replied quietly. Lavina's head whipped around so fast, she was shocked it did not fly completely off her shoulders.

"What do you mean he was dying?" she choked.

Elmo sighed and out of the corner of her eye, Lavina could see a sprinkling of lights from the town.

"Adam was diagnosed with stage four stomach cancer last year. Like many people who are facing death, he began to wonder why he had worked so hard without enjoying his life. He looked around at his expensive apartment and his fancy shoes and he realized that he wanted none of it. He wanted to live and live simply without the weight of the world upon his shoulders."

"But, Daed, he is never sick! He wakes at dawn and works all day. You cannot be right!"

"He won the battle against the cancer and he is in remission but it could return any time as cancer does. Adam vowed that he would not fall into the same trap which had run his life. He was sure that if he continued to live as he had, the cancer would return. Adam blamed his lifestyle for his poor health."

Lavina paused to register what her father had said, her mind spinning in dozens of directions.

"Is that why he put the time restriction on himself? He was worried that the cancer might return and he would not be accepted to join the church if he was sick?"

"We would never have turned him away for being sick, Lavina. In fact, we allowed for him to come into our fold because we were moved by his dedication to renouncing the outside world and accepting God's will. But yes, he wanted to ensure he was not brought in by pity but by virtue of earning his place."

Elmo stopped speaking and turned to Lavina, his eyes shiny against the black night.

"This is also why I asked you to teach him our ways," Elmo continued.

"Why?" Lavina was confused, her soul heavy with emotion.

"You have been questioning your path also. I know you have been ready to leave us since that boy broke your heart."

She was shocked by the revelation.

"How did you -?"

"Lavina, you forget that not only am I a minister in our district, I am also the father who loves you without end. When my children hurt, I become terminal. I found out the day after that girl showed up at worship. I cannot say I was upset at the time; I did not think of Eli as a good match for you but that was not my place to speak."

Lavina stared at him in awe. Any other father she knew would certainly have made it a point to object to the match but her father wanted her to learn from her own mistakes.

"I also knew that his true character would rear its ugly head and you would see him for the charming snake he is. You have always been a smart girl, Lavina."

He set me up to spend time with Adam so I would remember the goodness of living in this community. He hoped I would reconsider my actions before I did anything I would regret. He was right.

"Daed," Lavina asked tearfully as they drew near the hospital. "Is he going to die?"

"No, Lavvy. I believe Jacob Umble wrestled off Eli before too much damage was done. He was conscious when they took him and asking for you apparently."

Lavina's brown eyes were overflowing with tears.

He was asking for me.

His face was swollen with bruising and Lavina almost did not recognize him as she rushed into the room. She and her father had been in the waiting area since five o'clock in the morning and Lavina was a bundle of nerves.

"You may see Mr. Everly now, Miss Blauch, Mr. Blauch," the bored nurse intoned at eight o'clock. Lavina sprung to her feet but Elmo remained seated.

"Are you not coming?" she asked when she realized her father was not on her heels.

"I will go after you see him," he told her encouragingly. Lavina offered him a thankful smile.

"Danke, Dat," she whispered. He nodded.

"Oh!" Lavina gasped as Adam turned to face her. His eyes were red balls of puffiness and she could not see the vivid blue of his eyes.

"It looks worse than it is," he joked, his voice coming out in short rasps. Lavina swallowed the lump in her throat and hurried toward him.

"What did the doctor say?"

"He said I will heal and that next time I should try to fight back. I told him that I haven't done any training in REM sleep martial arts but I will consider it."

Lavina did not smile, a flash of fury toward Eli stabbing through her.

What a tough man, attacking someone when they are asleep.

She pushed Eli out of her mind and leaned forward to caress his battered face.

"When will you get out?" she asked, her hands shaking.

"They want to keep me one more night just to be sure but I'll be back tomorrow."

"What will you need? I will come to the Umble's every day and take care of you until you are well again."

Adam smiled weakly.

"Well, the doctor did say I needed one thing but it's big so I don't know – "

"Anything!" Lavina replied quickly. "What is it?"

Adam's hand reached up to enfold hers.

"He told me I needed the love of a woman named Lavina Blauch."

Lavina began to sob and she lowered her head against his chest.

"You already have that," she bawled. "I am not going anywhere."

THE AMISH WEDDING SEASON

DEIRDRA SCOTT

Chapter One

Wedding season. Every year it came and every year it sent a fresh wave of pain through the heart of Anna Harshbarger. Weddings were supposed to be joyful events, full of excitement as couples looked to the future but, for twenty-one-year-old Anna, they only brought to mind the pain of the past.

Sitting at the desk in her bedroom, Anna stared out the window and took a ragged breath. She was trying to spend her Sunday afternoon composing letters to her cousins in Pennsylvania, but her mind continued to wander to the church service that morning and the couple that was announced as engaged.

It had been two years since Anna had stood up in church with her boyfriend, Amos, and listened as the preacher announced their engagement. Those had been happy times – but the happiness had ended far too quickly. Anna had built up so many hopes and dreams, only to have them completely smashed and her heart left to suffer in the process.

Glancing down at the paper where she had started a letter, Anna noticed that the page was smeared with the tears that had started running down her cheeks. Grabbing the paper up, she wadded it into a ball and threw it in the trash can. She would wait to write her letter...she had no news to tell anyway. She had no husband of her own to brag on, no children with naughty antics to recall, no farm reports, and no exciting news about adding onto a house. Anna had absolutely nothing of her own.

Leaning her head against the oak desk, she sobbed, trying to muffle the sound by covering her mouth.

"Amos," She whispered between her sobs, "Why did you ever leave me?"

Anna had spent that year happier than any other. She had met Amos Yoder at a young people's picnic while visiting a near-by Amish community. He was more charming than any other man she had ever known. Days after meeting, he was already declaring his love to her, sending her constant tokens of his affection along with sweet poems and letters.

In hindsight, Anna could see that things had moved forward much too quickly. She had allowed herself to get caught up in a romance that accelerated before either of them had time to think.

When Amos asked Anna to marry him, they had only known each other for two months. Immediately after announcing their engagement in church, Anna could see a change in Amos. He suddenly became more distant and would go days without even speaking to her. Anna tried to convince herself that things would be fine once they were married and completely threw all her energy into planning the wedding.

The morning of the wedding, everything was prepared and in place...everything, that is, except Amos. He never showed up to the wedding and Anna was left alone with nothing but shame and a broken heart.

Closing her eyes, Anna tried to brush the memories out of her mind. No matter how much it hurt not to have a family of her own, she would never go through the possibility of the same pain again. She would not let another man hurt her, no matter what.

———————————-

"Mommy! Mommy, help me!"

Ben Eicher sat up straight in bed. Stumbling to his feet, he hurried to his little girl's room.

Lilly was sitting up in bed, her body shaking as she wrapped her arms around her knees. In the light of the moon, Ben could see tears running down her cheeks.

"Lilly," Ben hurried to her side and sat down on the edge of the bed, "*Ach*, child, everything's alright." Reaching out, he wrapped the four-year-old in his arms and pulled her tiny body close to him.

"*Daed...*" Lilly's voice was shaky as her tears continued to pour down her cheeks, soaking his nightshirt, "I dreamed about *Mamm*. She was in the water and it was covering her face. She needed help. She needed someone to come save her. She kept calling out for us, but we wouldn't go to her. *Daed*, we have to go find her now. We have to help her."

Words wouldn't come to Ben; instead, he just pulled the little girl tighter against him, wishing for all he was worth that he could make things better for her.

Pushing back, Lilly looked up into his face, her brown eyes pleading with him, "Daddy, can we please go see her? Please, Daddy! Please!"

Ben slowly nodded his head, "Lilly, I will see about that tomorrow. For now, you just have to go to sleep. You've got to get your rest."

Lilly's lips puckered up in a frown, but she slowly nodded her head. "Sing to me, Daddy," she whispered, leaning her head against his chest, "Sing me songs like Mommy used to sing."

Laying her head back against her pillow, Ben sang to his little girl until her tears finally subsided and she drifted off to sleep.

Taking a deep breath, Ben let it out slowly. Carefully pulling himself to his feet, he made his way back to the empty bed in his room. In the darkness, he closed his eyes and tried to sleep, but found himself invaded by miserable thoughts.

It had been a year since Lizzy had left home. Initially, Ben had hoped that she would come back once she had her fill of the *Englischer* world...but now, he realized it was impossible. Lizzy's choices had put a wedge between them that could never be removed. Their life together was over and, even if he was to kill himself trying to make things different, they could never again be together.

"God," Ben whispered into the darkness, "I know that I haven't been living the way that I'm supposed to. I know that I've made terrible choices...but does Lilly have to suffer forever for my mistakes?"

Reaching up to wipe away at his tears, Ben took a ragged breath. Maybe he'd gone too far – maybe it was impossible for life to ever be made right.

Chapter Two

Sunday morning church services were generally a pleasant time for Anna. She enjoyed the feeling of community as she gathered with the other Amish believers and let her heart soak up the message that the preachers delivered from the Bible. However, all pleasant feelings associated with church were now overshadowed by the loneliness of listening to new wedding engagements announced every Sunday morning.

The misery of sitting through the church service, dreading to see another happy couple step forward made Anna feel almost nauseous.

That bright Sunday morning was no different. Anna sat through the service in total sorrow. Rather than paying attention to the message or the people around her, she found herself staring at her hands which were folded in her lap, silently praying that she could make it through the service without getting sick.

"Why Lord?" She found herself whispering to herself, "Why did you allow me to go through so much pain? Why did you bring Amos into my life? I feel like I'm completely ruined for anyone. I can never bring myself to love again and I will be alone forever. I simply don't think anyone can change things for me...not even you, God."

Beside her, Anna's sister Beth leaned close to her ear and asked, "Are you okay?"

Anna nodded her head, bracing herself for the worst as the preacher wrapped up his message.

"I now have a wonderful-*gut* announcement to make," his words caused Anna to close her eyes and tightly grip the edge of the hard wooden pew.

"We have a new family in our community!" Preacher Joe continued, "I'd like everyone to meet Ben Girod and his daughter Lilly."

Anna let out a sigh of relief, thankful not to be faced with greeting another happy young couple. Opening her eyes, she looked up to see a strange Amish man stand and face the congregation; at his side stood a little blonde haired girl with huge blue eyes. Anna found her attention drawn to this handsome new-comer and, even when he sat back down, it was hard for her to look away.

With dark brown hair, brown eyes, and a strong chin, it was obvious that Ben was a fine figure of a man. But something about Anna's attraction went deeper than simply his appearance. Looking at him, it almost seemed that she could sense a common bond that connected their very souls.

"Anna, Anna," The sound of Beth's voice brought Anna back to her right mind and alerted her that everyone was starting to file out of the church for a community picnic.

Walking with her family, Anna felt her heart leap when her *daed* stopped to talk to the man the preacher had introduced as Ben Girod.

"Hello there!" Mr. Harshbarger said with a smile, throwing a hand in Ben's direction, "I'm Levi Harshbarger. It's good to have you in the community."

It was easy to see that Ben wasn't good with meeting new people as he shifted his weight from one foot to another awkwardly. Anna noticed his little girl stood close to his side, certainly not a fan of strangers either.

"It's good to know you," Ben finally announced as he reached out to take her father's hand for a shake, "I just moved here last week and I only know one or two families."

"What kind of work do you do, Ben?" Anna's father asked.

"Mostly roofing work," Ben explained, reaching down to give his daughter a reassuring pat on the head.

"Oh, that's good!" Mr. Harshbarger said with a smile, "We've got a bad leak in our kitchen, but I haven't had a chance to work on it yet. Would you mind coming by to check on it sometime soon?"

Ben was quiet for a moment and then glanced down at his daughter, "I could come tomorrow morning, but I'll have to find someone to watch her..."

"*Ach*, no problem there!" Anna's *daed* insisted, "I've got two daughters still at home – they can watch out for her."

Slowly, Ben agreed that he'd come to look at the roof the next day. Rather than staying to eat with the community, he excused himself, explaining that he needed to get on home.

"Ugh," Beth whispered to Anna as the girls followed their parents out of the house where church had been held and into the yard for a delicious meal of homemade potato salad and fried chicken, "I'm sorry, but I don't look forward to having Ben Girod around our house! I've seen happier men at funerals."

Anna tried to smile, but could hardly force it. Deep in her heart, Anna recognized something about Ben that mirrored herself. Rather than dreading to see him, Anna was frightened to realize that she actually looked forward to meeting the handsome stranger once more.

"Anna Harshbarger!" She muttered to herself as she scooped a pile of gooey potatoes onto her plate, "Have you lost your mind? And just after you swore you'd never look at another man again."

But, despite scolding herself, Anna still kept counting down the hours until she would once again be able to steal a glance at Ben.

Chapter Three

True to his word, Ben arrived at the Harshbarger house early the next morning. Anna and Beth had just finished with the breakfast dishes and had started on a new quilt to sell at the market in town.

When Anna heard Ben's buggy pull into the yard, she felt her heart leap and quickly peered out the window.

Anna's *daed* met Ben at the front door.

"Come on in," Mr. Harshbarger invited, opening the door a bit wider.

Standing close at Ben's side was his little daughter. The child was wide-eyed and looked terrified as she struggled to stand closer to her father and wrapped her arms around his legs.

"Anna, come here!"

At the sound of her name being called, Anna took a deep breath and stood up from the quilting frame. Suddenly, she found herself feeling overwhelmed by an uncomfortable awkwardness as she made her way across the floor.

"Anna, you remember Ben Girod from church," Her father's words caused Anna to look up and give a nod. Ben nodded back and Anna couldn't help but notice his gaze rested on her, "He's going to be looking at our roof and I need you to keep his little girl occupied while he's busy."

"Lilly," Ben leaned down to talk to his child, "I've got to work. You can go play with this nice lady while I'm busy."

The child's face clouded over and tears threatened to pour down her cheeks, "No, Daddy, don't leave me."

Lilly looked so pitiful, Anna's heart was moved with compassion. Bending down to the little girl's level, Anna whispered, "If you want, we can go out to the barn and see the new kittens. Would you like that?"

Reaching up to wipe at her tears, Lilly slowly nodded her head.

Abandoning her sewing, Anna took the child out to the barn where they looked at the newborn kittens, hunted for eggs, and made a fort out of hay bales. Although Lilly was shy and sad initially, she quickly changed as she started to have fun.

Ben surprised them both when he interrupted their game of hide-and-go-seek.

"I'm done for now," he told Anna, giving her a tap on the shoulder as she leaned forward to look in an empty horse stall. Raising his voice, he called out, "Lilly, time to go home!"

Lilly climbed out from under a blue tarp and started to shake her head, "No, Daddy, please, not yet! I'm having so much fun!"

To Anna's surprise, the little girl ran to her side and flung her arms around Anna's waist, "I'm having fun," she continued to plead, "Can't I stay longer?"

"We'll be back tomorrow," Ben informed her, "I've got to finish up once I buy some supplies. If Miss Anna wants to play with you more then, she can."

Lilly started to wipe tears from her eyes but obediently went to the house to wash her hands and get ready to start home. Anna found herself feeling completely ill-at-ease alone with Ben in the barn.

"Thanks for spending so much time with her," Ben finally announced as he took the toe of his boot and scrapped a line in the barn's dirt floor, "Lilly's been having a rough time of it lately. She's had too much loss for a girl her age. She misses her *Mamm*...this was good for her."

Anna could only nod. She wasn't sure what had happened to Ben's wife, but was happy to have helped the sweet little girl.

Watching them drive away, Anna found herself anxious for the next day so that she could once again see Lilly...and Ben.

Over the next few days, Ben continued to work on the house and brought Lilly with him. Anna realized that she was becoming far too attached to the child. Something about the little girl's presence filled a void that Anna didn't even realize was in her heart.

Surprisingly enough, Anna couldn't seem to keep her eyes from glancing in Ben's direction either. Watching him working on the top of the house, she found herself admiring his strong work ethic and desire to make every detail perfect.

"I've got to go into town to get some nails," Ben announced one morning as he crawled down from the ladder, "Lilly, do you want to come with me and get some ice cream?"

Glancing at Anna, Lilly called back, "Can Anna come too? I only want to go if Anna can come!"

Ben smiled and slowly nodded, "If she wants to come along she can."

Anna instantly felt uncomfortable as Lilly grabbed her hand and pulled her toward Ben's buggy.

"*Ach*, Lilly," Anna mumbled, "I'm not sure if I should go..."

Lilly smiled, "Everyone loves ice cream, Anna. Come on...my *daed* will pay!"

Climbing onto the buggy seat, Anna made sure that the little girl was positioned between herself and the handsome man who was working on their house.

While Anna had seen a lot of Ben from a distance, she had not had many chances to talk with him or learn much about his character. While he had always seemed distant, uncomfortable, and sad, it all changed as they traveled down the road together. The entire trip Ben pointed out animals in the weeds alongside the road, told stories from his childhood, and made both Anna and Lilly laugh at his silly jokes.

During their time in town, they stopped at the ice cream store and got delicious chocolate cones, and then made a quick run by the hardware store.

Full of ice cream and exhausted from the trip, Lilly fell asleep on the way back home, leaving Anna and Ben completely alone. To Anna's relief, conversation continued to come easily as they talked about Ben's plans to renovate the house he had recently purchased, different people within the community, and the school that Lilly would start once she turned seven-years-old.

There was something about Ben that melted the ice on Anna's heart. She couldn't ignore the fact that he looked at her with a certain softness in his eyes. Obviously, she wasn't the only one who was feeling a good share of attraction.

"Why did you decide to move here?" Anna asked.

Ben clucked his tongue at the horses, "After all that happened, we needed a change. I hoped moving would make it possible to start over fresh."

Anna reached out to stroke a strand of hair that was peeking out from beneath the sleeping little girl's black prayer bonnet.

"Tell me about Lilly's mother," Anna asked softly, "What happened to her?"

Ben took a deep breath and shook his head slowly, "That's a part of the past I don't really want to talk about...Let's just say that she and I both made a mess of things. Now she's gone forever."

Anna had so many questions she wanted to ask, but she wasn't sure if Ben would appreciate hearing them. It felt so good to have a man by her side...a man who was looking at her like she was valuable and treating her like he truly found her important. If she pushed him to talk about something he wanted to keep secret, perhaps he would leave her like Amos had left.

"Fair enough," Anna finally conceded.

"What about you?" Ben took a turn asking, "Surely you've had men in your life before. I can't believe a pretty girl like you hasn't had her share of beaus by now. Why aren't you married?"

The words stabbed Anna like a knife. Suddenly, she found herself feeling uncertain and anxious to change the topic. If Ben realized that she had been jilted at the alter, he might realize that she was defective and unimportant.

Anna shifted her weight uncomfortably on the bench and shrugged, "I'm like you, Ben – I'd rather not talk about my past. You're not the only one who has a secret to keep."

Ben nodded his head, "I suppose that's fair enough, too."

They both laughed and Ben took a deep breath of the fresh spring air, "Well, I suppose I'd better get you on home. It's too late to finish the roof tonight, but I can probably wrap it up tomorrow."

Something about the words brought a fresh sense of pain to Anna's heart. The idea of having Ben gone seemed so terrible.

"Anna," Ben was silent for a minute before he finally said, "I have enjoyed today. And I've enjoyed working at your house. I...would you be willing to think about continuing to see us after my work there is finished?"

For years, Anna had sworn that she would never consider falling in love with another man; however, as soon as the question was out of Ben's mouth, Anna quickly exclaimed, "Yes!"

Completely unknown to Anna, Ben had practically held his breath through their entire trip into town. Realizing that the roofing job was almost finished had been awful. Over the past few days, he had felt his heart getting constantly more and more soft toward Anna; watching her play with his little girl and the way that Lilly had grown to love the Amish woman had started to melt down the walls he thought were safely established around his emotions.

After their fun trip to town, Ben realized that he didn't want to let Anna go. Of course, he would have to eventually, but not yet.

Chapter Four

Ben hadn't been joking about continuing to see Anna. As soon as the roofing job was finished, he offered to take her out to dinner along with Lilly at a fancy restaurant in town. Over the next few weeks, they continued to see each other frequently.

Although Anna truly enjoyed Ben's company, the closer they grew to each other, the more uncomfortable she began to feel. Each time they were together, she looked for signs that he truly did care about her. When he seemed distracted or distant, her feelings were instantly hurt; however, when he showed signs of tenderness, Anna discovered that she was even more ill-at-ease as she dreaded falling in love only to be jilted once again.

"When's he coming again?" Beth asked as she and Anna worked together in the barn one afternoon.

Anna gave a shrug, trying to appear as if she didn't understand the question, "Who?"

Beth tossed a handful of straw in her sister's direction and laughed, "Anna, you're so silly. Ben, of course! You're out with him all the time. When is he coming back?"

Anna took a deep breath as she spread some fresh straw out in one of the calf pens, "He said we'd go out riding tonight."

"*Ach*," Beth let out a happy sigh, "I feel like my sister may not become the old maid of the community after all! And here I thought that I'd have the chance to get married first!"

Listening to Beth's happy chatter brought a strong heaviness to Anna's heart.

Setting her pitchfork aside, Anna leaned back against one of the large posts in the barn and took a deep breath, "I'm not sure about any of that, Beth..." She let her voice trail off as she noticed her younger sister's happy smile turn into a frown.

"Anna?" Beth bit down on her lower lip and made her way to Anna's side, "What are you talking about?

Anna slowly shook her head, wishing that she had kept her thoughts to herself.

"Don't you care for Ben?" Beth asked, putting her hand on Anna's shoulder.

Suddenly, Anna felt her eyes start to fill with tears, "Oh, Beth, of course I do! Each day we spend together, I find my heart softening more toward him. I love him so much. The idea of spending life without him is misery to me."

Beth threw her hands up in surprise, "Then what's the problem?"

Anna shook her head and grabbed for her pitchfork, suddenly anxious to get back to work and push her miserable thoughts aside. Stopping in the midst of her work, Anna turned back to her sister and announced, "I think he'll leave me, Beth."

While it felt good to get her fears out in the open, it felt like she had released a floodgate of emotions. Anna felt her chin start to quiver and hot tears ran down her cheeks.

"Sister, surely you don't think Ben is like that!" Beth exclaimed.

Jutting out her lower jaw, Anna looked at her little sister and boldly announced, "I didn't think Amos was either."

Beth opened her mouth and then closed it. Obviously, she was unsure of what to say.

There was nothing to say, Anna reasoned to herself. Amos had left her – it only made sense that, if she was not important to him, she wouldn't be important to Ben either.

By the time that Ben arrived that afternoon, Anna was almost sick with worry. Talking to Beth had made her feel worse than ever. It seemed that speaking her fears aloud made them all the more likely.

For the first time since they started going out together, Ben came without Lilly. Not having the little girl along made Anna feel ever more uncertain. Climbing up on the buggy seat beside Ben, she wondered if this was a sign that he was ready to end their developing relationship.

"Lilly is staying with one of the neighbor girls," Ben explained as Anna settled down at his side, "I thought we could use some time to talk together."

Anna nodded slowly, suddenly feeling sick at her stomach.

As they started out the driveway and onto the country road, conversation seemed to come slowly. Ben took Anna into town where they picked up a hamburger at the local diner. Although it was obvious that Ben had wanted to spend time alone with Anna, he said nothing out of the ordinary; instead, he slowly began to drift into familiar topics such as things that Lilly had done that day and a funny story about one of his new calves. While Anna breathed an internal sigh of relief that he wasn't heading into unpleasant territory, the fact that he wanted to discuss something private with her put her on pins and needles.

When Ben finally took her home, Anna could contain her curiosity no longer.

"What did you want to talk about?" She finally asked, her bluntness surprising to her own ears.

Glancing in Ben's direction, she saw a softness in his eyes that leveled out some of her fears.

Ben cleared his throat, obviously nervous.

"Anna," Ben took a deep breath before he went on, "My Lilly needs a mom. Except for me, she's all alone in the world and, as a roofer, I spend a lot of my time doing dangerous jobs. If something was to happen to me, she would be totally by herself. I know that you're not keen on getting married after...whatever happened in your past, but I also know that you need a place of your own."

Anna looked down at her hands and began rubbing them together. She thought she knew what Ben was getting at, but she wasn't sure if she wanted to hear it – not this way.

"There aren't very many women my age who aren't already married or at least seeing someone," Ben announced, "And I don't have any faith in younger girls to take *gut* care of Lilly. I trust you, Anna. Would you consider marrying me?"

Anna swallowed the lump that was forming in her throat. All her hopes of ever finding romance with Ben Eicher seemed to suddenly fall apart. He didn't love her – she was just the solution to a problem.

Slowly, Anna nodded her head, "I guess it's something to think about. How soon do you need my answer?"

Ben gave a shrug as he looked out across the fields, "I dunno...would a week be long enough?"

Getting down from his seat, Ben hurried to help Anna to the ground so she could start the short walk to her parent's house.

"Ben," Anna sighed deeply and looked up into his eyes, trying to hide the pain that she felt in her heart, "I don't need to wait. You're right, I need a place of my own. I'll marry you."

Giving a slight nod, Anna forced a smile, "I'm very tired, so I'd better get inside. Goodnight." Taking a deep breath, she bit down on her lip and started up the walk, trying her best to contain her emotions until she was safe in her own bedroom.

As he watched Anna walk away from his buggy, Ben felt his heart sink. He had planned for the night to go so much differently. Although he knew that their relationship was new and a proposal was truly premature, he had hoped that Anna had at least started to care about him as more than a friend.

Ben had seen the doubt in Anna's eyes. Sure, she had agreed to marry him, but it was with the same enthusiasm that one would agree to a root canal. He had hoped that maybe she was starting to develop feelings for him but her lack-luster acceptance of his proposal proved that wrong.

"She'll leave you, Ben," he heard a teasing voice play through his mind, "She'll be just like Lizzy. She already doesn't care about you...what are things going to be like once she actually *knows* you?"

Shaking his head, Ben climbed back onto his buggy and started the journey toward his home and little girl.

Asking Anna to marry him had been a mistake, and now he found himself unsure of how to make his wrong right.

Chapter Five

Anna spent her night crying into her pillow. *Ach*, if it hadn't been bad enough to be the only one without a boyfriend, this had to be so much worse! Over the past few weeks, Anna had started to care so much for Ben; she found herself thinking about him throughout the day and dreaming of a time when he might come to develop even the smallest feelings for her. Now, her tiny ray of hope had been shut out. Ben had only pretended to be interested so that he could find a mother for his daughter. The fact that she was still unlovable broke a part of Anna's heart.

The next day, Ben didn't come to see her. When he finally came by two days later, it was simply to check on the roof to make sure it was still sturdy after a hard rain.

"Ben's here!" Her father announced.

Anna was standing at the sink, washing some breakfast dishes. While a part of her wanted to run out and see him, she restrained herself and stood her ground. If he wasn't going to see her, she wasn't going to throw herself at him either. She'd made a fool of herself with Amos – she wouldn't be doing that with Ben!

By the time Anna was done with the dishes, her *daed* was leading Ben into the kitchen.

"Anna," Mr. Harshbarger spoke up, "Could you get Ben some sweet tea? I'm sure it's hot up there on that roof!"

Anna nodded slowly and hurried to fill a glass with ice at their cooler. When she returned with the drink, she passed it to Ben without even looking at him.

"Thanks," Ben muttered before he continued talking to her father about the roof.

Was this how Ben was going to treat her now that they were engaged? He'd hardly speak to her! Anna shook her head to herself and reached up to wipe a tear away from her eye. It reminded her so much of Amos and the way that he had acted after she accepted his proposal.

Ben's behavior was more than Anna could take. She excused herself quickly and hurried outside to feed the chickens.

Standing in the Harshbarger's kitchen, Ben felt his heart grow heavy when Anna quickly left the room. He already felt uncomfortable enough to be there and Anna's behavior made things even worse.

If he had questions before, it was obvious now: Anna wanted nothing to do with him. The kindest thing he could do would be to quickly break off their engagement before it could cause even more pain. It would be better to end things now than to wait until they were announced in church.

After telling Mr. Harshbarger goodbye, Ben made his way to the chicken coop where Anna was tossing feed on the ground.

Just looking at her broke Ben's heart. She was so beautiful. Ben had hoped that she had grown to care about him but, the more time that passed, the more he realized that was impossible.

"Hello there," he managed to whisper around the lump in his throat. Anna looked up from her work in surprise and gave an awkward nod.

"Anna," Ben shook his head and kicked at a clump of dirt on the ground, "What I asked the other day...well, it was ridiculous. I'm sorry I even brought it up. I don't know what I was thinking. Obviously, things would never work out. I think it is best if we just forget I ever talked about that, and stop seeing each other."

The words had been hard to get out. Ben looked down at his boots and swallowed hard.

"Yes," Anna finally announced, "I think that would be best too."

With a slow nod, Ben whispered "Goodbye" and started toward his buggy.

As soon as Ben was out of sight, Anna left the chicken pen and hurried upstairs to her bedroom. Her tears were flowing freely and she didn't even try to stop them. Slamming her door shut behind her, she threw herself across her bed and buried her face in her quilted comforter.

"Anna," she could hear Beth's voice outside her bedroom door.

"Go away," Anna whispered, but Beth didn't listen; instead, she opened the door and walked into the room.

Anna pulled herself into a sitting position and began wiping furiously at the tears on her cheeks.

"Anna," her sister sat down beside her and put an arm around her shoulders, "What has happened? Did you and Ben fight?"

Anna shook her head, "No...no fighting," she managed to sob, "We just broke up. He said it was over and I said okay."

"Are you really going to just let Ben get away from you?" Beth asked in surprise, "*Ach*, you're a strange one, Anna! I've always been able to tell that you love him...but he probably can't! Why won't you just admit it to him?"

Anna shook her head sadly, "I can't stand to be jilted again, Beth! If that happened, I think it would just kill me. You don't know what it's like to be left standing at the alter...the shame and the heartache and the disappointment. When that happened, everything in my life felt like it was crashing down around me. I'm just now starting to pick up the pieces...I can't do it again."

Beth took a deep breath and sighed, "Anna, you're tricking yourself if you think you've been getting better. For the past two years, I've watched you caught up in this maze of misery...and only when Ben showed up did it start to look like things were going to change. He put a spark back in your eye, Anna! I watched you fall in love with him, but I've also watched you work hard to try to hide it. Maybe the poor man simply doesn't think you care."

Anna rolled her eyes, "Beth, you're full of craziness....I practically threw myself at him!"

Beth raised an eyebrow, "Truly? Anna, at any point did you truly make him feel confident that you cared? Or were you too busy trying to protect yourself from pain?"

Her sister's words suddenly cut deep. Beth was right; Anna realized that she had been so busy trying to keep herself from being injured by Ben, that she had never thought that she might be hurting him.

"Talk to him, Anna," Beth pleaded, "Just take a few minutes to talk to him! *Ach*, we both know you'll regret it forever if you don't!"

Slowly, Anna nodded her head. She wasn't sure how she could find the strength, but it was time to stop hiding.

Chapter Six

Anna took Beth along with her to watch Lilly while she talked with Ben. When they pulled their buggy up to his small house, Anna felt like she would lose every bit of nerve she possessed.

Ben came to the front door, total confusion spread across his face.

"Anna!" Lilly exclaimed, running out into the yard to meet them, "Anna, I've missed you so much!"

Anna took the little girl in her arms and hugged her. "Play with Beth for a while," she whispered to the child, "I've got to talk to your *daed*."

Lilly reluctantly lead Beth out to the barn to look at the calves.

"Anna..." Ben's voice trailed off slowly, "I'm not sure..."

"We need to talk," Anna said with a sigh, "Can I come in?"

Ben stepped back, allowing her into the kitchen.

"Ben," Anna sat down at one of the chairs and took a deep breath, "You once asked me why I wasn't married. The answer is simple but it hurts to talk about. I was supposed to get married, but my beau ran off the day of our wedding. I swore to myself that I'd never let another man into my life....and then you came along. Ben, I've come to care for you. My sister tells me that I've been cold and distant...I understand if you don't want to marry me, but you need to understand why I act the way that I do."

It was in the open now. Anna let out a deep breath and sat back in her seat, suddenly feeling like the weight of the world was off her shoulders.

Ben had eased down in a chair across from her. He looked down at his hands and slowly whispered, "Anna...it's not that I don't care for you...."

"Then what is it?" Anna asked, suddenly feeling angry.

"I'm scared!" Ben exclaimed, slapping his hand against the table-top, "*Ach*, you're not the only one who got jilted. Lizzy...my Lilly's *mamm*....the same thing happened with her. After five years, she left me and found another man....along with a life away from everything we had together."

Anna's eyes got large, "What do you mean?"

Ben ran his hands through his hair and closed his eyes in mixed shame and pain, "I have made some stupid mistakes, Anna. Up until the last year, about all my choices were stupid, to be honest. Lizzy was a wild girl from our community who couldn't seem to keep her feet in the Amish ways. From the time we were kids, I was fascinated by her. She represented everything exciting in my life. Growing up, she would constantly manage to run away from the community...sure, after a few months, she would come dragging back home, but she was as wild as a deer. I wanted her to love me, Anna. We started courting at the young peoples' gatherings. I'm afraid that things went much too far much too fast. Lizzy became pregnant soon after we got together. I wanted to get married – everyone in our community expected it, but Lizzy could hardly stand the idea. She never wanted to be tied down to anyone or anything. Since we were both teenagers and neither of us had been baptized into the faith, no one could make us do anything – we were still on our *rumspringa*. For a while, I ran away with Lizzy and we lived together in the *Englischer* world. But once Lilly was born, I knew I wanted her to grow up in the faith, even if I wasn't living it. Lizzy and I moved back to the Amish community and continued to live together but never got married. The Bishop would try to talk us into getting married and settling down, but there was no convincing Lizzy and, since we weren't members of the church, we had no real rules to live by."

Anna felt like her eyes were so big, they might just jump right out. The words that Ben was saying came as such a surprise. "When did you marry her?" She finally asked.

Ben shrugged his shoulders, "We never did get married. It was a terrible life. I knew that things needed to change, I knew that I needed to get right with God, but I wasn't sure how when I was living so opposed to his ways. Over the years, Lizzy would leave me a lot. She'd run off to the *Englischer* world again and leave me alone with Lilly for months on end. The last time, she ran away for good." Ben took a deep breath and looked down at his hands, "She got a new boyfriend that wasn't raised Amish. She moved into his apartment. I went to try to talk to her so many times, but she had changed...in my heart, I realized that she would never come back home. It became obvious that she was gone for good when she had a baby with her new boyfriend. She went to the court and signed Lilly over to me. I'll never forget standing in that courtroom after she signed the papers. Here she was, the girl who I had loved since I was a boy, and she came to my side to tell me that things were over for good."

"When Lizzy left for good, I realized it was time to make a change. I went to the church leaders and I apologized. I got baptized into the faith and totally changed my ways. I moved Lilly to this area so that we could have a fresh start." Ben looked down at his hands and started absentmindedly picking at a fingernail, "Since I had never actually been married to Lizzy, the bishop decided that I could go on and live my life as a single father...and get married if I ever wanted."

Daring to look up at Anna, Ben whispered, "I never thought I would want to. I truly thought that women were a thing of the past for me."

"And yet...you asked me to marry you," Anna managed to say. Looking into Ben's eyes, it was hard to imagine why he had even asked her. After all that he had gone through, all of his terrible mistakes and the consequences of his bad choices, it would seem that a relationship would be something he would want to avoid.

"You changed something in me," Ben managed to say, his voice sounding shaky, "You brought back what I thought was gone for good. I felt love in my heart once more...but, after so much happened, I wasn't sure what to do. I was so worried about getting hurt, I kept doing stupid things."

Anna laughed and nodded her head, "*Ach*, me too!"

Their eyes met and Anna found herself feeling embarrassed but also full of joy.

Reaching out to take her hand in his own, Ben whispered, "I don't think we need to get married any time soon. Obviously, we've got a lot of hurt between us that needs to be resolved. But, I don't want to run from my feelings any longer."

"I don't either," Anna admitted, tears of joy beginning to run down her cheeks.

"I love you, Anna Harshbarger."

"And I love you!"

Reach out to embrace one another, the two people that never thought they would experience love let the ice melt from their hearts as they basked in its healing glow. It would take time to work through all the hurt that they had endured, but together they would see a day when they felt free to love each other completely.

THE BABY BUGGY

SARAH TORRES-THOMAS

Chapter One

"Alright, Kip. Time to go into your stable," Aaron said to his horse as he gently tugged at its reins. Aaron walked besides Kip quietly but quick in pace as the sky above was becoming dark with rain clouds. He could already smell the scent of rain in the air; a scent he was all too enamored with. It reminded him of the day he and his wife, Sarah, were married over seven years ago, in the middle of a thunderstorm. The claps of thunder during their Amish wedding ceremony were so loud that at times, they were unable to hear the words spoken by the bishop. For over seven years, Aaron and Sarah had attempted to conceive a child. Sadly, with no success—until now. Many months they waited to see the results of their work but Sarah's cycle never ceased; the dreaded cycle that filled them both with feelings of incompetence and disappointment. The fact that their friends got pregnant on the first time sometimes gave them a tiny bit of envy, although, they were always happy for anybody who was able to enjoy such a blessing. A few weeks ago, Sarah's dreaded cycle did not reset and her monthly visitor missed its appearance. When this occurred, their mind did not automatically think about the cause being a pregnancy. Although they had always remained hopeful, it simply did not seem possible. They were convinced that their last attempt had been successful when Sarah, who was always healthy as a horse, became extremely ill. A pelvic exam performed by their Amish settlement's midwife confirmed that Sarah was indeed with child.

As Aaron removed the bridle from Kip's head he thought about how life would change once their child was born and was filled with gratefulness. All of those years of pain from being unable to procreate vanished the moment they found out about their baby. Aaron was definitely excited about what the future held for him and his growing family. He picked up a brush from a pail and brushed Kip's mane. When he was finished, he draped a green blanket over the horse's back. Then, he quickly made his way back inside the farmhouse expecting Sarah to greet him so lovingly as she usually did. As soon as Aaron shut the door behind him the rumbling started from the skies. The fire was going in the fireplace but Sarah was nowhere to be seen or heard.

"Sarah?" Aaron called out to the silent house. He went to the kitchen thinking Sarah was still preparing dinner but she was not there. He called out again. The house stood eerily quiet, something was wrong—he knew it. He slowly started to make his way around their home, opening doors expecting to find Sarah. He called out to Sarah, this time more frantically. It was highly unusual for Sarah to not be home at this time. Finally, he stepped into their bedroom which was located towards the very back of the house. The bathroom door was slightly opened and he could see dim candlelight. Aaron pushed the door open to find Sarah sitting with her head in her hands on the bathroom floor in her nightgown. She was crying.

"Sarah, what's wrong?" Aaron asked her bending down next to her. Then, he saw. Sarah was sitting in a pool of her own blood.

"Oh, god, Sarah. What happened? Did you hurt yourself?"

"Something is wrong with the baby. All of a sudden I just started bleeding profusely," Sarah said through sobs. Aaron put his hands on her face and realized that she was soaked in sweat.

"You're burning up. We have to get you to the midwife right this instant," Aaron said as he tried to help her up. Sarah let out a bloodcurdling cry.

"Okay, okay," Aaron said, "I'll be back, Sarah. Don't move. I'm going to bring the midwife. Please, stay here." Aaron bolted out the house in the pouring rain. He arrived at the midwife's house and pounded on the door. A man, the midwife's husband, opened the door with a bothered look on his face.

"Why are you knocking like so?" the man asked, "We are in the middle of dinner and you come knocking like a madman. What do you want?"

"I'm so sorry, Jett. Bertha must come quickly, something is very wrong with Sarah and the baby," Aaron told him catching his breath. At that moment, Bertha, the midwife, came to the door.

"What's going on with Sarah?" She asked worriedly.

"She's bleeding and in pain. Please, Bertha. Come quick!"

By the time Aaron and Bertha made it to the house, they can hear Sarah's screams coming from inside. They carried Sarah to the bed and laid her down. Bertha sent Aaron to the kitchen to gather supplies for her examination.

"Sarah, I think you are in labor," Bertha told Sarah.

"No, this can't be happening. This baby is not due for another twenty weeks or so," Sarah cried.

"Aaron, I think you better get to a phone to call for an ambulance. It seems like she's hemorrhaging and you know our supplies are limited here at the settlement. If we want her to be safe, we have to get her to a hospital quickly." The events following Sarah's predicament were a blur to Aaron. He remembered the hospital and the doctor telling him about his child's death. He felt a sense of relief when the doctor told him Sarah was recovering and that she would be well physically, but was hit with pain like from a gunshot wound when they also explained that Sarah had an emergency hysterectomy. If their chances of having a baby were little before, their chances would definitely be impossible for the rest of their lives. The rest of that night and even the following days were blurry and muffled. Aaron didn't recall doing anything but sit next to his brokenhearted wife's bed.

Chapter Two

A year had passed since the loss of their unborn child and of any hope they had of growing their family with children of their own. Other members of their Amish settlement would sometimes ask why they didn't consider adoption. Truthfully, they had but it was much too expensive and did not have that amount of money. For the most part, people did not mention the loss to them. It seemed to have been forgotten by the other members but never by Aaron and Sarah. On the anniversary of the unborn child's death, they went out into the fields to pick flowers. They were making an arrangement of yellow, purple and red wildflowers.

"We should start heading back soon," Sarah said looking up at the sky, "it seems that rain clouds are rolling in."

"You're right. Let's just cut a couple more and we can get going," Aaron replied.

"How fitting, right?" Sarah asked him. He was kneeling cutting stems and her question made him freeze. He turned to look at her. Sarah was looking at the bunch of flowers she cradled in her arms.

"I'm not going to cry," she said.

"You should, if you feel like it," Aaron told her placing his hands on her shoulders.

"No, that won't bring our baby back now, will it?"

"It won't but we should not keep our emotions all pent up." Sarah walked over to Kip and began loading the flowers they had collected into the buggy. Aaron followed behind her and before helping her up onto her seat he wrapped his arms around her.

"You're the strongest person I know," he told her, "I'm so glad that *you're* still here. You were part of our child and you're still here. I'll always have our baby with me as long as you're living with me, too."

"That's beautiful. What a nice way of putting it, Aaron. Thank you," Sarah replied with a smile. They finished loading up their buggy and soon, they were on their way back home.

That night Sarah baked some decadent desserts in celebration of their baby's short life. The baby had died but it had also lived and was very loved in that time span. In order to lift their spirits, they also played a few board and card games. It was obvious in the way that the couple interacted and spent the time in each other's presence that after all they had gone through, they were very much in love. After their fun-filled night, they joined in bed and said their good nights. The thunder had begun and the rain was starting to land heavily on their rooftop. A few hours after they had gone to sleep, they heard a loud crash; anybody could have confused it with the wind causing an object to fall or with thunder. Aaron laid in bed listening to the sounds coming from outside when he heard a neigh.

"We secured Kip's stable right?" Sarah asked still half-asleep.

"I'm sure we did." Aaron said as he got up to find his coat. There was another clash outside. He thought that maybe the thunder had spooked Kip and he tried to come looking for them.

"If you're sure, why are you going outside in the rain?" Sarah asked in the dark.

"Just for sanity's sake!" He replied shutting the room door behind him.

Once he got outside he realized the horse that neighed was not Kip. There was a black horse with a buggy tied to it standing by Kip's stable. The buggy was damaged and Aaron could tell that the horse had run right through the fence from the picket still stuck in the wood. Aaron ran to the horse to see if people had been hurt in the buggy. The horse trotted away from him in fright. He let Kip out of the stable to see if it would calm the other horse down. Kip followed the horse and eventually, the horse allowed Aaron to get close enough. From the outside, there didn't appear to be anybody in the buggy. Aaron figured that maybe someone had left their horse outside during the storm and the horse took off in search for shelter from the thunder. He walked up to the horse and stroked its wet face telling it that it would be okay. He walked behind the buggy and opened up the small white curtain. At first glance, it appeared empty but in the darkness he could make out a bundled up yellow blanket. He reached for it and he froze when he felt a soft body, still warm. He gently picked it up with two hands and pulled it closer to himself for inspection. He moved the blanket a little to see who or what was wrapped in it. Aaron stood there looking into the face of a baby not older than a few weeks. He immediately went into protector mode; wrapping the baby to shield it from the rain and ran as fast as his legs could go back into the house where Sarah was waiting for him in the living room. Sarah walked over to Aaron when she saw how concerned he had returned. Her initial thought was that Kip actually had escaped his stable and had run off or gotten injured but then she saw the bundle he was carrying.

"What's this?" Sarah asked but she could already tell that it was a baby from its shape.

"A horse came crashing through the community fence looking for shelter. This baby was in the buggy but nobody else was around," he answered breathlessly. Once Sarah realized that this baby could be critically hurt she gently picked it up from Aaron's arms.

"It's warm so that must mean it is alive," Sarah said examining the baby's face. She gently laid it on the couch and unwrapped the yellow blanket. The baby was wearing a white silky nightgown. Sarah undressed the baby and examined the limbs one-by-one. At the same time, she was in awe of the smoothness of the baby's skin and its ability to sleep through all of the commotion.

"It smells a little—odd," Aaron said with his nose in the air.

"We should change the baby to prevent a rash. Please bring me some cloth and pins," Sarah instructed her husband. Slowly the baby began to rustle awake and it was at this time that Sarah began to feel nervous. She was afraid the baby would not like them or want its parents and make a big fuss for their neighbors to hear.

"I'm going back to the buggy," Aaron told Sarah as he returned with the cloth and pins.

"What for?" Sarah asked.

"Well, people are going to ask questions when they find that a foreign horse and an empty buggy appeared in our fields. I also want to see if whoever had this baby left behind any baby supplies in there. The baby will wake soon and it will be hungry."

"You have a good point," Sarah said as she slowly removed the baby's diaper. It was in that moment when they discovered the baby was a girl.

"Oh, Aaron. It's a beautiful baby girl," Sarah said happily.

"Yes, she is quite beautiful," Aaron replied as he put his coat back on. Kip and the strange horse had walked back to the stable by that time. It was still raining pretty heavily so Aaron quickly untied the horse from the buggy and put it in the stable next to Kip. There was not much room for two horses but they would only be in there for one night since Aaron planned on finding the owners the next morning. Aaron dried off the horse with a towel before searching the buggy.

Inside of the buggy, Aaron found shopping bags with food and supplies. Thankfully, among the groceries was a small tin of powder formula for the baby. He hadn't spotted the bags during his initial search because the baby had diverted his attention. Aaron also found a small purple coin purse in one of the shopping bags. Upon opening the purse, he found no money but he did find a photo less identification card belonging to a woman, presumably the baby's mother or guardian. Aaron had so many questions about the entire situation. Where are the baby's parents? Why was the horse so startled? Why did the parents leave behind their baby and groceries in a buggy? Answers were going to have to wait. The only thing that mattered was that the baby was well taken care of and safely returned to her parent's arms. Aaron put the groceries back in the bag and left them there but he took the baby formula with him. When Aaron entered the house again a few minutes later, Sarah was still on the couch with the baby girl. She had already changed her diaper and had wrapped her in a fresh blanket.

"I found formula," Aaron said holding up the tin.

"Oh, good!" Sarah exclaimed.

"We might have a small problem, however," Aaron continued, "We don't have any bottles to put her formula in." Sarah told him otherwise. After their baby had died, they put away all of his belongings and kept them in their bedroom closet. It was not many things; a bottle, a few blankets and onesies. That was all that was left of that time in their lives when they were parents and Sarah could not bring herself to give away those belongings. Following the directions on the tin of formula, Aaron made the baby's bottle.

"Alright, here we go," he said handing the bottle to Sarah who was cradling the baby ever so affectionately. She put the nipple to the baby's lip and surprisingly, she took it right away. Sarah cooed at the baby as she watched her eat and make the cutest sounds.

"We should go to bed now. It's really late and we have to wake in the morning to ask around the community for the parents of this baby," Aaron told Sarah while he stroked the baby girl's head. They made their way back to the bedroom and put the sleeping baby on their bed.

"You can sleep on the bed with the baby," Aaron told her, "I'll sleep on the couch so I can hear if anybody comes looking for her." He walked over to the bed and sat down. He watched as Sarah caressed the baby's rosy cheeks and ginger hair. She traced the baby's palms with her finger and whispered sweet things to her trying to comfort her even though the baby was nowhere near distressed.

"What should we call her?" Sarah finally asked.

"Well, I think we should wait for her parents to come find her and we can ask for her name then."

"What if they don't come?"

"They will. Who would abandon their child this way? We wouldn't, would we? It wouldn't make sense."

"I hope they can leave her with us," Sarah told him.

"Sarah, that's a horrible thing to say. This baby needs her real parents. I hope they come as soon as possible; I'm sure they are missing her miserably."

"I guess," Sarah sighed. Aaron had already taken notice of Sarah's interactions with the baby. Sarah was already beginning to make the baby her own without even considering that the baby's parents could have showed up right then and there. However, it could not be helped—after all, Sarah never got to hold her own baby. Aaron refrained from saying anything else about the situation and left her to cuddle the baby in peace.

Chapter Three

Aaron was in a deep slumber when he was suddenly startled awake by a loud knocking on the door. He could tell from the dim light coming through the curtains that it was still a very cloudy morning. He opened the door to find two men and a woman standing on the porch.

"Yes, how can I help you?" He asked groggily.

"Good morning. We've come to ask about this run-down buggy by your stable. We heard a commotion last night and were wondering if that's the reason why," one of the older men said to him. Aaron went on to explain about the events of the night but for some reason, left out the details of finding a baby inside of the buggy. The woman began to whisper to the other man standing beside her.

"Is something else the matter?" Aaron asked curiously.

"We think this buggy might belong to an Amish couple from another community who were found murdered on the side of the road a few hours ago." Aaron was in complete disbelief.

"What else do you know?" Aaron asked them hoping they could give more information about the events of last night.

"That's pretty much it. They are not from our community or from the community a few miles away. We don't know much about them," the woman revealed.

"Are the police involved?"

"Yes, they are and they said the couple's baby is missing, too." Aaron tried his best to not look suspicious.

"Oh, wow. That's terrible," he told the people.

"Yes, it truly is. We must pray for this couple, whoever they are, and for their baby to be safe wherever it may be."

"Yes, we shall pray. Thank you for letting me know about the buggy. I am going to get in touch with the police as soon as I get dressed," Aaron said shutting the door.

"Well, if *that's* not suspicious," Sarah told Aaron. She was standing in the hallway as he spoke with the neighbors and she had heard everything. The baby was sound asleep bundled in her arms.

"What?" He asked.

"You basically shut the door in their face," she scolded.

"What would you have rather me do? Bring the baby to the door? I should have done that. This baby is not ours. Why are we hiding her?"

"We can't give her back. Her parents are dead, you heard. She needs loving parents. We can be that for her."

"We don't know if she has other family. What if she has siblings or grandparents? We can't rob them of her that way. I think this is kidnapping, Sarah."

"It is not kidnapping! She's a blessing. Don't you see, Aaron? Why would she appear on the anniversary of our child's death? God has surely sent her to us."

"God did not have her parents killed like animals out by the road to give us a baby. Please, be rational."

"We did not kidnap her. You found her. Why has nobody come looking for her?"

"I don't know. If her family comes looking for her, we *will* give her back."

"But she needs parents—,"

"Enough!" Aaron interrupted, "We are not liars and we do not keep things that are not ours. We are returning the baby and that's final."

"I'm not going to let this baby live without her mother. I'm her mother now!" Sarah exclaimed as she stomped back into the bedroom. Aaron could hear her crying from where he stood in the living room. He didn't know what to do. He felt as if taking the baby girl from Sarah would be like their baby dying all over again. He left her alone for the rest of the morning while he prepared himself to call the police over to return the horse and buggy. Aaron wanted to find out if the police knew who the couple was and if they had any family. He knew that the longer that Sarah was with the baby, the more they would bond and the harder it would be to return her to her family. Even though, regardless of when they returned her, Sarah would still be devastated.

Aaron phoned the police and let them know that the horse and buggy belonging to the couple had ended up in their Amish community in the middle of the night. The department sent the detective in charge of the homicide case along with forensic analysts. He went outside to meet with the detective, a short bald man, and told him what had occurred.

"There was nobody here with the horse?" The detective asked Aaron, looking him right in the eyes.

"No, sir. I did not see or hear any person around here. I just heard the horse crashing through the fence. When I came out, there was nobody around."

"Did you touch the buggy?"

"Yes, sir. I searched it to see if I could find who it belonged to. I did happen to find a coin purse with an identification card but I left it where I found it."

"Okay, well we are going to be a while here on your yard while we collect any evidence left behind by the perpetrator," the detective told him.

"Yes, yes. Take all the time you need. Detective, I heard that the couple also had a baby with them the last time that they were seen," Aaron said.

"The last people to see the couple alive were the owners of a convenience store not too far from here and they said they had a newborn with them but we have not found any baby."

"I see," Aaron said, "if you do find this couple's family—would it be possible for you to give me their contact information?"

"What for?" the detective asked.

"Oh, you know," Aaron answered, "we would like to pray with them and offer them any help or anything else they might need."

"That's very kind. We'll let you guys know once we find the community they were from."

"Okay, Detective. I will be working in the field just right over there. If you need anything else from me, please let me know." The men said their goodbyes and Aaron went straight to the field start on his daily tasks. He almost went to warn Sarah to stay inside the house and hide the baby but he knew Sarah would be more than just careful in order to keep the baby longer. He was quite distracted throughout the day, however, fearing that someone from the community would come inform him of the police taking his wife away for holding a baby hostage.

Aaron returned home after his work day right before sunset. He could smell the aroma of the warm dinner Sarah had prepared before he even entered his home. He found Sarah in the room with a freshly bathed baby. The baby was wide awake looking around the room. Every time that Sarah spoke to her, she cooed in reply. The dampness of her skin and freshness of the air made her cheeks and nose rosy. Sarah quickly wrapped the baby in her long sleeping gown to keep her warm.

Her curls became wild after they air dried from the bath, giving her a rather comical look. Aaron looked at the baby's big gray eyes and unruly hair—he couldn't help but to laugh. Sarah and the baby both turned to look at him.

"I'm sorry," Aaron said trying to calm down, "She looks so funny."

"She does, doesn't she?" Sarah cracked a smile, "She sure is the cutest baby I've ever seen." Aaron could see the infatuation in his wife's eyes; the way she held the baby and cared for her revealed a tenderness she had been wanting to express to their own baby. Aaron had no doubt that Sarah would have been the most loving mother of them all. The baby was beginning to get drowsy and a bit fussy from hunger.

"I'll go make a bottle," Sarah told Aaron, "Do you mind holding onto her?" Aaron nodded his head.

"Wait, it's been years since I've held a baby. Maybe it's not a good idea," he told Sarah. It was true that he had not held a baby in a long time and that made him nervous. However, he was more afraid of falling in love with the baby girl that he knew they could not keep. He was afraid that holding a baby momentarily would bring back all those bitter thoughts and emotions about never being able to hold a child of his own.

"Don't be a scaredy cat," Sarah teased. She showed Aaron how to make his arms comfortable to cradle the baby and gently laid the baby on him. While Sarah was in the kitchen preparing the baby's meal, Aaron stared at the baby's features. He wondered what his child would have looked like full-term. Would it look like him or like Sarah? Would their baby have had curly hair like Sarah or straight like his? He gave his index finger to the baby and she gripped it tightly.

"Whoa, you're a strong little lady aren't you?" He said to her.

"Do you want to feed her?" Sarah said handing him the warm bottle. Aaron looked at Sarah unsure about what to say. He wanted to repeat to her that they had to find the baby's family but a part of him loved being in that moment with both of them finally taking care of a precious human being—theirs or not. The baby eagerly drank her formula and in the process, fell asleep. They laid her down on the bed and quietly exited the bedroom to have dinner themselves.

The two sat at the dinner table quietly—wanting to express themselves yet not wanting to fight. They both wanted a baby but Aaron never imagined it would happen like it did. He did not want either of them to get into trouble with the law for keeping the baby.

"I had so much fun with the baby today," Sarah started, "I think we might have to make a formula run to the store tomorrow morning. I never knew a human so small could eat so much. She smiled at me a couple of times today; I almost melted." Aaron felt sad about how smitten Sarah was with a child who was not hers. Despite Sarah's stubbornness in regards to the situation, Aaron felt it was his responsibility to speak some logic to her.

"I think tomorrow we should go to the police and tell them we found the baby," Aaron told her. He didn't want her to be angry with him but he knew it was inevitable now.

"But they'll take her," Sarah says.

"She's not ours. We have to do things the right way, Sarah. God's way. I don't think he would approve of us hiding the baby this way."

"God sent this baby to us. I know he did. He wants to help me heal from the loss of our baby by having me be the mother of this beautiful baby girl."

"No. Our child died. That must mean that we are just not meant to be parents. It was not in God's plan for us."

"How can you say something like that? Are you saying that I would not make a good mother? Why do women who abandon their children get to bear them and not I? Because I'm not good enough?"

"You know that is not what I mean. Do you really want to rob her of a family? What will we tell her when she asks when she's older? You have to think about the future, too."

"Her parents are dead. God chose us to care for her. She could end up in foster care of be adopted by horrible people. Don't squander this blessing. I just know we won't ever get a chance like this ever again," Sarah said as her eyes began to cry. Aaron grabbed her hands and held them up to his face.

"I know you are still hurting, my love. I also lost a child last year, too. But this is not the right way to do things. We have kept her by lying. Do you plan on hiding her for the rest of her life? You hide her because you know we are not supposed to have her. Please, I am trying to protect us." Sarah sobbed quietly, not wanting to wake the baby. She knew her husband was only trying to do the right thing.

"If she is meant to be ours, God will show us the right path," Aaron assured her.

Chapter Four

After dinner, they went to bed and laid alongside the baby. Sarah let the tears silently roll down her face as she lamented having to say goodbye to the baby. They both caressed her tiny head and velvety cheeks in awe of her perfection. How Aaron wished he could heal his wife's broken heart. He didn't care that his was also broken; he just wanted her to be happy again. At the same time, he was also feeling pained from having to give up the baby. For the first time since finding out about her parent's deaths, they also cried. They were heartbroken for the orphaned baby; for the possibility of her being a child of a system who doesn't strive to provide the best life for all the children in their care. At that moment, they hoped that if they could not be her guardians, that she still had family out there somewhere.

The next morning, they were both woken up by someone knocking on their front door. Aaron got up to greet whoever it was.

"Good morning," said the detective standing on the front porch of their farmhouse.

"Good morning, Detective. What can I help you with today?"

"We found a relative of the couple," the detective said handing him a paper with the baby's parents community address.

"We have still not found the baby, however," the detective continued. It was then that Sarah stepped into his view holding the baby girl in her arms.

"This is the baby you have been looking for," Sarah said with teary eyes and a heavy heart. Sarah and Aaron were then taken to the police department in order for them to give their statement of the night that the baby was found. They were under investigation for more than a few hours but were finally released at the end of the day. There was nothing to prove that they had ever been involved with the couple's homicide and after all, they had rescued the baby from possible harm on that stormy night. The detective came out of his office holding the baby girl.

"We are going to return the baby to her community," he told them, "It's obvious that you really care about this baby. Would you like to come along?" Aaron and Sarah both nodded. They sat in the backseat of the patrol car cuddling the baby and saying their goodbyes. Upon arriving at the baby's community some 45 minutes after leaving the station, they saw that people were already waiting for her return. The detective came around to open the door for them and they stepped out. They looked at the faces of all the people praying for the baby's safe return. Both of them expected the reunion to be loud and booming with cheers and shouts of joy but it was eerily quiet. A younger woman stepped forward pushing the wheelchair of an elderly woman. Her hair was silver and she had glazed eyes.

"Anna, your great-granddaughter has been found. They have brought her back home," the young woman said to the old woman.

"I want to hold her," the woman said holding out her arms. Her voice was dry and scratchy. Sarah got closer to the woman and placed the baby in her hands. The woman brought the baby close to her face and took a deep breath. Her hands traced the baby's hands and face. She broke down and began to cry.

"Thank you, thank you," she told them both as she kissed the baby's forehead.

"We want to apologize for not returning her sooner," Aaron told her.

"We are sorry," Sarah added, "we were immediately enamored with this sweet girl of yours. We didn't want our time with her to end but she belongs with you."

"Thank you for keeping her safe," the woman told them, "Tell me, do you have other children?"

"We do not," Aaron replied, "My wife, Sarah, had complications during her pregnancy last year and we lost our first and only child. We are unable to ever become pregnant again."

"Do you want to take her back with you?" the old woman asked.

"What do you mean?" Sarah asked.

"I am very ill and don't have much time to live. I am not in the best condition to be raising a child as I am also invalid and am blind. While I do love this child with all of my heart, I cannot do much else for my great-granddaughter, Meredith."

"Are you her only relative?"

"Yes. Her mother was my granddaughter whose own mother died during childbirth. After I am gone, she will have nobody."

Sarah and Aaron stayed at the community talking with the old woman for many hours. By the time they had come to an agreement, it was already late at night so the members of the community offered them a place to stay for the night since the road was not considered safe for the time being. They learned many details of the baby's, Meredith's, family history—one that they had planned to tell her about as she grew up. As the months went by after they had returned home, they would occasionally return to visit the old woman along with baby Meredith until the old woman was no more. The woman had not lied when she said she had little to live. Although a part of their heart would always be missing from the loss of their premature child, Meredith completed their lives in unimaginable ways. Sarah had always known that she was sent by God to restore their lives. Meredith was their daughter even if not by blood. They loved her like they would have loved any child that came from their own flesh and blood. Whenever there was a thunderstorm, they were reminded of the night that Sarah gave birth to death but it also reminded them of the night that they met the most beautiful baby of all.

Pride Before the Fall

"Mom! The sauce is on fire!"

Andrea glanced up from her lesson plan and gasped as she realized her son was right to be alarmed; the red sauce had bubbled over onto the burner.

"Matthew get away from there!" she yelled as her six year old son hurried fearlessly toward the stove. She was instantly around the kitchen island, removing the sterling silver vessel with a gloved hand.

"I said get away from there!" Andrea repeated as she and threw some baking powder on the stove.

"That was cool," her son said.

Andrea's heart continued to pound as she forced a smile at her child.

"I was trying something new. Rose flambé; it's French Italian fusion."

Matthew looked uncertain but eventually grinned back at her once he recognized the near catastrophe had been averted.

"Sounds delicious," he declared.

The side door at the kitchen opened and Andrea's husband strolled in.

"Dad!" Matthew said, running to hug his father.

"Hey Matty! How was your day? Learn anything interesting in school?" Philip put Matthew into a playful headlock before releasing him and giving his wife a kiss hello. Andrea wiped her hands on her apron and cupped her husband's face affectionately.

"Nope but Mom is cooking French fission," Matthew announced. Andrea laughed, turning back to her dinner preparation.

"Fusion," she corrected. Philip raised an eyebrow and took in the unsightly mess of the kitchen.

"Sounds...interesting," he answered dropping his briefcase on the table next to the mount of paperwork which Andrea had been attempting to tackle.

"Still at it?" he asked, gesturing at her pile of schoolwork. Andrea nodded and rolled her eyes.

"I would have been done hours ago but Ariel called and kept me on the phone for two hours."

"Oh? How is my favorite sister in law these days?" Philip asked, snatching up an uncut carrot and plopping into a chair, crunching into the meaty vegetable.

"Very well, apparently. Dad agreed to officiate her wedding and she can't stop talking about wedding flowers."

"Your dad agreed to marry her? Even though it's her third time down the aisle?" Philip was surprised. "That's very magnanimous of him."

Andrea nodded in agreement. Her father had made no secret of the fact that he did not approve of Ariel's multiple marriages. He was a very conservative pastor and followed a highly traditional view in almost all aspects of life. Yet, at the end of the day, he was a father above all else and his priority was to his family, even if his youngest daughter changed husbands like seasonal footwear.

"Are we going to this one?" Philip asked. Andrea groaned inwardly. She knew that he was about to start on a speech about Ariel making a mockery of civil unions and Andrea really didn't feel like hearing it that evening. She had far too much work to do. She was already behind on her lesson plans because of the upcoming wedding. She couldn't afford to spend more time listening or talking about Ariel.

"Of course we are," Andrea replied, annoyed, tossing the salad. "She's my only sister."

"Well if we miss this one, we can always catch the next one," Philip joked. Andrea scowled at him.

"What a thing to say, Phil. Ariel has had a hard time in relationships. It isn't her fault that the men she chooses make her miserable. She is trying to find happiness. It is our duty as her family to support her and hope she finds whatever she is looking for in life." To her surprise, Philip looked thoughtful and nodded in agreement.

"You're absolutely right, honey. Everyone deserves to be happy. Sometimes that doesn't fit in to what other people think is right but that's okay. Right kiddo?" Philip turned to smile at his son who was flipping through a comic book on the living room floor.

"Right!" Matthew agreed without raising his eyes. Andrea placed the salad bowl on the table and turned back to retrieve the pasta. *Well that's a change from his usual fire and brimstone approach,* she thought. Philip and her father were two peas in a pod. Both had rigid, conventional ways of thinking and opening their minds had been a concept Andrea had forsaken many years earlier. It was easier to listen to them talk about the wrongs of others than attempt to instill some empathy in either one. Needless to say, they enjoyed each other's company immensely. This is why Andrea found her husband's words so abruptly refreshing. But she had to admit, lately he had been acting much more lenient than usual toward topics which would once send him on diatribes for hours.

"The lord has blessed us with the ability to forgive and understand others," Philip intoned as Andrea ushered their son into the dining room. She bobbed her head in agreement.

"Yes, it is a wonderful thing to see the good in others," she told Matthew. Matthew groaned and laughed.

"Aw, mom, you're such a pastor's daughter. You always see the good in everything!" Andrea was inexplicably touched by her son's words. He had no way of knowing that she strove to be positive and her one hope was that Matthew would grow up to be optimistic also. Life was hard enough without focusing on the bad. *Not that you have much to complain about,* Andrea reminded herself. *You married your dream man, you work in your dream job and you have the dream child. Life is pretty darn good from where you're sitting.* In fact, Andrea had never struggled greatly. Being the eldest child of an esteemed pastor, she had been brought up in comfort and security, exposed to the wonderful aspects of small town living. She had met Philip in high school and they had married as soon as they had graduated college. One year later, Matthew had blessed their lives. Seven years after they had tied the knot, they were both thriving wonderfully in their careers, Philip as an accountant and Andrea a ninth grade history teacher. They owned a split level house, two cars and a Golden Retriever named Binky. It was as though God had handpicked her to have a storybook life and Andrea could not have been more content, appreciating the small things every single day. She tried very hard to instill those values on her family also. She hoped that Ariel would find the same peace of mind with her new husband. She found herself thinking it was a blessing that Ariel had not yet had children. Andrea found herself staring at her own freckle faced son and wondered how someone so innocent could endure the trauma of a divorce. *Who knows? Maybe Ariel would have stayed with one of her ex's if she had a child.* She was appalled by her own thought. *Of course, that is a terrible reason to stay with your spouse if you are unhappy enough to end your marriage.* Andrea sat down that the head of the table, directly across from Philip. *Thank God that Matthew will never have to go through anything like that.*

"Matty, do you want to say grace? Maybe something about being grateful tonight?" she asked, pushing the dark thoughts out of her head. Matthew cleared his throat and the three bowed their heads.

"Mom? Mom! I'm home!" Matthew was met by silence as he entered the house. A quick glance around confirmed that his mother was not on the main floor but her silver Toyota was parked in the driveway. Typically, she was not home so much before him and the babysitter, Veronica would be there to greet him. That day, however, only Binky came flying out of the kitchen, followed by their surly tabby,

Potato. Binky waged his tail and licked Matthew's hand and the boy absently scratched his golden head.

"Mom?" Matthew called out again. "Mom are you here?"

There was still no response and suddenly the six-year-old was hit by a feeling of apprehension. He slowly climbed the stairs, still yelling for Andrea. He listened for the sound of running water, thinking that perhaps she was showering but as he reached the landing of the second floor, the door to the bathroom was wide open and empty. Binky whined, demanding Matthew's attention but the child continued toward his parents' bedroom, ignoring the excited animal on his heels. The door was slightly ajar and he pushed it open. For some inexplicable reason, he felt that something was terribly wrong.

"Mom?" he almost whispered as the door fell away. Laying on the bed, fully clothed atop the blankets, was his mother, wide eyed, staring at the ceiling. His heart racing, Matthew rushed to her side.

"Mom, are you all right?" he choked. To his overwhelming relief, Andrea turned her head slightly toward her son. But as soon as the sense of security fell, it was replaced by concern as he realized his mother's eyes were bloodshot and her cheeks tear stained. He climbed onto the bed.

"What happened? Are you okay? Do I need to call 9-1-1?" Matthew fired off, terrified, his hands shaking at her. Andrea shook her head slowly and wiped at her gentle hazel eyes, sitting up slowly. She sniffled and as she came into an upright position, three sheets of paper fell to the floor. Matthew reached for the handwritten note but Andrea took his hands before he could move.

"Everything is okay," she told him, her voice raw. Then she hugged him with so much emotion, Matthew was afraid he would break under the embrace. When she released him, she stared into his eyes, identical to hers and said nothing even though he stared at her expectantly. Finally, she found the words she needed.

"Matthew, I'm so sorry, honey but your father is gone."

The letter had been hand delivered to her by a man she did not know during Andrea's free period. She had been in the teacher's lounge, sitting among some of her peers enjoying a coffee when one of her co-workers called her outside. The fellow said not a word but handed her an unsealed envelope and walked away before she could ask him any questions. After the strange man had left without introducing himself, Andrea had stared at the piece of paper for what seemed like an hour before slowly rising and walking out of the school without saying a word to anyone. She had somehow managed to drive home although she had no idea how she had made it there without getting into an accident for she had no recollection of the ride. She had made her way up the staircase and into the master bedroom, shoes still on and fell into her bed. Only then did the tears start to flow. They did not stop until she heard the front door open and Matthew call out her name. The note had been written in a black pen with what Andrea thought was lovely calligraphy. It read:

Dear Christopher,

As you know, I have been unhappy for many years now. I can only assume that you have been also but since our interactions seem to have reached a stalemate, I have no idea what you are thinking or feeling anymore. I have found solace in the church over the last months, again, something I have no idea if you know but my faith in God has helped me through the difficult times in our marriage. I always believed that once we married, we would remain together forever but the past years have made it increasingly difficult for me to honor my commitment to you. Still, I believe that we would have stayed in this farce of a relationship if I hadn't met Philip.

Philip is a devout man of God who has been an incredible support to me since I joined the church. He has spent countless hours comforting me, wiping the tears from my eyes and simply listening to me. It's been so long since anyone has actually listened to me, Christopher. He reminds me of what it was like when you and I were young and in love. It is really no surprise that I found myself looking to him amorously. To my absolute disbelief, he loves me too. Of course neither of us planned it this way as he, too, is a married man but life is full of unexpected changes. Chris, Philip and I have decided to start a life together away from here. This is not a decision we have made lightly. I do not expect you to understand or forgive me as I imagine I am basically a stranger to you now, despite our almost twelve years together but I do ask you one thing; please seek out Philip's wife, Andrea. She is a teacher at Thomas Edison High School in Springfield. Philip does not have the heart to break hers, even in this form. You must let her know that he is not coming back. It is a lot to ask, I know but if you do not, she will only imagine the worst has happened, potentially starting a police investigation. Please find it in your heart to alleviate this woman's suffering.

I wish you only the best, Christopher. I am sorry this is the path God intended for us but He does work in mysterious ways.

Yours No Longer,

Dianne

At first, Andrea was sure the three page letter was a horribly cruel joke, orchestrated by one of her co-workers. Some of the teachers with whom she worked had a slightly askew sense of humor but the more she thought about it, the more she realized that all of the signs were there; the odd late nights at the church, the strange phone calls in the night and Philip's suddenly one hundred eighty degree turn in personality. Andrea reread the pages over and over, looking for some clue as to the psychology of the woman who had won her husband. *Won? Did I really lose?* Andrea asked herself sadly. Dianne claimed to be a religious woman, one who put her faith in the church and God. *And she ran off with Philip, a married man with a child. How dare she imply that this was God's will? She blatantly disobeyed the laws of God and of moral decency.* Andrea was furious. *And what about Prince Philip? He didn't even have the gall to tell her himself that he was abandoning her and their son? Who did you marry? How could you have not foreseen this?* She lay there, her blood boiling, tears flowing, lost, helpless and screaming inside. She had never been so devastated. When Matthew came home, a smidgen of hope sparked within and she briefly thought it might have been Philip. But a well honed intuition told her that Dianne was very real and her husband would not show his face in that house for a long while, if ever again.

Now, staring at her son's confused face, she inhaled and braced herself for the painful conversation that was about to ensue.

"Dad is dead?" Matthew choked, tears welling up in his gold flecked irises. Andrea immediately recognized her mistake and shook her head vehemently.

"No! No! No!" she said, hugging him close. She felt Matthew exhale in relief.

"What do you mean he isn't coming back?" her son pressed, drawing back. "Is he okay?"

Andrea realized she was still holding her breath.

"Yes, honey…" Andrea stopped herself. She looked at the wide eyes of innocence and a blanket of woe wrapped around her. Her whole world had been shattered in one afternoon by some stranger with a letter. She couldn't do the same thing to her son. It was her job to protect him from harm and darkness. That was her role as a parent. She discarded the thought she had formed in her head and started again.

"Your father has… gone on a mission to…Africa…for…a long, long time," Andrea stuttered. She was not a natural liar. She had never really had cause to indulge in deception. But at the tender age of six, Matthew did not recognize when he was being lied to and his face fell further.

"When did he leave? Why didn't he say good-bye?" he asked, tears filling his eyes. Again, Andrea fumbled for the words, wishing she knew exactly what to say to make his loss easier.

"He wanted to, Matty, but it was an urgent mission and he got called right away. The church needed him." Matthew fought to blink away the tears and nodded. Andrea's heart broke even further. *He's trying to be brave,* she thought, trying not to bawl herself. She hugged him again.

"Can I call him?" Matthew asked, reaching for the landline telephone on the night table. Andrea stopped him and shook her head.

"Not right now," she said shakily. She needed more time to think through what to tell her son.

Matthew nodded.

"Okay, mom. I'm sorry. You must be upset too. You probably got called to go too but had to stay because of me." Andrea thought she may have died, she was so grief-stricken at that moment. Matthew was clearly tormented by the news but worried about her feelings. She couldn't believe the amount of love in her son. She shook her head again and forced a smile.

"Matty, there is nothing in the world I'd rather do than be here with you. You are my mission from God," she told him. Then she forced herself off the bed.

"Let's order a pizza for supper," she announced. Matthew smiled through his sadness.

"We'll be okay, mom," he told her, slipping his hand into hers and following her out of the bedroom. *Yes we will,* Andrea thought, squeezing his small palm. *God will never throw more at you than you can handle.*

God's Pitching Arm

Andrea sat nervously in the outer office. On her right, a Senior with spiky black hair and eight earrings in one ear was popping gum belligerently and on her left, a mousy Freshman was reading "A Tale of Two Cities" while tapping her foot. The noises were grinding on Andrea's already taut nerves but she said nothing to the girl or the boy. She felt like she was a schoolgirl in trouble as she waited for the principal to see her but she knew it was much worse than a scolding or detention waiting for her beyond the glass doors. As she wiped her sweaty palms on her black tailored pants, she watched as Principal Jameson waved her in with an old, weathered hand. The gesture itself was casual but Andrea could read the grim expression on her superior's face. *So I was right,* Andrea thought as she slowly rose and walked into the office.

"Sit down, Andrea. Do you want some coffee?" Principal Jameson asked her, motioning toward the chair before him. Andrea shook her head and sat, obligingly.

"How is everything going?" he asked pleasantly but Andrea was not in the mood for small talk.

"Sam, just cut to the chase. I'm being fired, aren't I?" Jameson blinked at her blunt question and then sat heavily in his high backed swivel chair.

"You know that there have been major cut backs, Andrea," he began with his well rehearsed spiel but she cut him off.

"I don't need you to sugar coat it, Sam," she snapped with more anger than she intended. It was no surprise that she was sitting there. She had only been teaching at the school for three years so she was definitely on the low end of the food chain. The cut backs were not an excuse; several teachers had been laid off in the past months so she had been prepared for "the talk" but it didn't make the blow any less painful. She had built up a reputation as an easy going teacher. Students fought to get into her classes and she had hoped that her character would have stood for something during this crunch but apparently it had been written in stone already. Still, Andrea had to try. This was what had been keeping her going the past weeks since Philip had left. She had thrown herself into teaching and her students.

"Sam, I am not the newest teacher here. Surely Mr. Cameron and Ms. Pascal have less teaching experience than me. They're both straight out of college." Sam nodded slowly, he seemed reluctant to speak.

"Yes...that is true, Andrea," he said. Andrea arched an eyebrow.

"But?" Sam seemed to be gathering his courage. He cleared his throat.

"Normally, you would be right. We would be apt to lay off one of the newer people but off the record, Andrea, your performance has suffered greatly since your husband left." Andrea was dumbfounded. She had been the ideal teacher, starting early, staying late. *What is he talking about?* She decided to ask.

"What are you talking about? I have been going out of my way around here!" she was almost yelling. The students in the outer office looked up in surprise. Andrea immediately lowered her voice.

"I mean, I just have been throwing myself into work," she continued lamely. Sam nodded sympathetically through his spectacles.

"I have noticed you're working extra the last few weeks. Maybe you're working too hard," Jameson told her softly. Andrea was completely perplexed by what she was hearing. She waited for him to continue.

"You have been launching into diatribes in your classes."

"Diatribes?" Sam looked extremely uncomfortable.

"You have been lecturing the children on history..."

"That is what I am being paid to teach!" Andrea was becoming annoyed.

"Yes, you're employed to teach history, not tell the students to be wary of history repeating itself. You're giving lessons on trust and quite frankly, Andrea, you're sounding cynical. While I know your personal circumstances, the children are beginning to skip your classes and I've been getting calls from the parents about your behavior." Andrea felt herself flush a deep red as she suddenly understood what the principal was saying. *Oh my, he's absolutely right! I have been bringing my personal anguish into the classroom! Why didn't I see it before?* She turned to Sam, her eyes huge with comprehension.

"I had no intention of sounding so bitter, Sam! I can stop. I just needed someone to show me the error of my ways!" Andrea pleaded. "Please don't take my job from me."

Again, Sam sighed and wagged his head.

"It's a done deal, Andrea. It's already gone to the board. The time off will do you good. You can gather yourself and as soon as something else in the district comes available, you'll be a shoo in. I promise I will give you an excellent reference. Your track record has always been stellar with us." With that, Sam rose to his feet, indicating no room for argument and moved toward the door. Stunned, Andrea also rose. A part of her wanted to scream out from the injustice of the situation but a sound part of her held back for she realized what he said was the truth. The tentacles of Philip's betrayal stretched beyond the scope of what she could have imagined.

Darkest Before the Dawn

"Mom! Aunt Ariel is here!"

Ariel followed her nephew into the house and gasped aloud.

"What?" Matthew asked. "What's wrong?"

Ariel quickly recovered from her shock and grinned briefly at the boy.

"Nothing, nothing. Where is your mom?" Matthew shrugged and returned to the living room floor and his video game. Ariel cringed as he stepped over empty chip bags and plopped onto a filthy pillow. The normally pristine house was a pig sty.

"Andrea?" she yelled. "Where are you?"

"In the kitchen," came the muffled reply. Ariel followed her sister's voice into the back of the house. She stepped over piles of laundry but whether they were dirty or clean, Ariel could not decipher. As she walked into the rear of the home, she paused, narrowing her eyes. Her sister sat at the table in the eat-in kitchen, a bottle of Merlot half finished in front of her. It was two o'clock in the afternoon.

"Hey! What are you doing here?" Andrea asked with feigned happiness. Ariel walked in slowly and sat down beside her sister.

"You haven't returned mine or dad's calls in a week, Andrea. I wanted to make sure you were okay. Matty said you got laid off."

"Meh, I'm fine. I'm enjoying the down time," Andrea replied, taking a sip of wine. "Want some?" Ariel scrunched up her nose.

"No...have you eaten anything today?" Andrea looked pensive for a moment and then shrugged.

"Probably. We have pizza. You want some?"

"Andrea, go have a shower. I'll take you and Matty out for dinner." Andrea shook her head.

"No thanks. There's a movie on Netflix I'm dying to watch. Hey, how are the wedding plans going? You must be getting excited for the big day!"

"Okay. Paul and I have been doing our pre-marriage counseling at the church with dad. Maybe you should go to the church. It can help you through this," Ariel told her, gently.

"Oh yeah! God has been so helpful the past few weeks. I should go visit him and thank him for all he's done around here. Also you should tell Paul to be careful – the church has a way of stealing husbands," Andrea laughed. Ariel could not believe what she was hearing. Andrea's faith had always been unwavering and her disposition had never been negative. Ariel tried another approach.

"Andrea, you need to get yourself together. You can't sit around drinking and living like a barn animal. You have a son to worry about," Ariel told her sister sternly. Andrea's head whipped up and she glared at her sister.

"Excuse me if I don't subscribe to your domestic bliss newsletter, Ariel. What marriage is this for you again?" Hurt, Ariel stood up, tears springing to her eyes.

"Andrea, it is always darkest before the dawn. Please think of Matthew. He's lost his father. He needs his mother."

"Thanks, Dr. Phil. And thanks for stopping by!" Andrea waved drunkenly at her sister, refilling her glass and defiantly taking a sip, eyes narrowed. *What does she know?* Andrea asked herself as she watched her sister spin on her heel and leave. She ignored the sense of guilt she was feeling at speaking that way to someone who loved her so dearly.

"Matty! What do you want on your pizza tonight? The usual?"

"Hi dad!" Andrea was still in her bathrobe, digging around in the mailbox when her father pulled up in the driveway. The pastor climbed out of his Cadillac and seemed to be analyzing the scene before him.

"Hi, sweetheart. How are you?" he asked slowly, strolling up the stone walkway. He leaned in to give her a kiss on the cheek. She smelled as though she had no showered in days but the Pastor admitted to himself he was relieved he did not smell alcohol on her. It was almost four o'clock in the afternoon, however and Andrea was wearing flannel pajamas underneath her tattered robe. Her hair was uncombed and he was sure that she had not brushed her teeth all day. The pastor had been very concerned after speaking with Ariel the previous day so he had decided to visit his daughter after work.

"Meh, you know. I'm still here. How are you?" Andrea ushered her father into the house and he saw the state of disarray that his younger daughter had spoken of during their phone conversation. He wisely made no comment.

"Is Matty home yet?" the Pastor asked brightly. Andrea shook her head and picked up a pile of dirty socks and a pizza box from the sofa to make room for him to sit.

"Not yet. He will be soon, though," she answered. "Did Ariel send you?"

The Pastor shook his head but Andrea smirked disbelievingly.

"I'm okay, dad. You should be focusing on Ariel's wedding for Saturday. I promise, I'll take a shower," she joked but suddenly her eyes clouded as she realized she would be required to bathe in the upcoming days. She crunched up her nose.

"I haven't seen you at church in a while," her father commented, ignoring her attempt at subject changing. Andrea shrugged.

"God and I aren't really talking these days," she said. "We had a disagreement. He seems to think that ruining my life is funny. I don't really see it that way."

The Pastor grimaced at her flippant tone.

"God works –"

"Yep, in mysterious ways. I know. Thanks. Well if he has anymore mystery to throw at me, he knows where to find me." Her father gritted his teeth. This was completely uncharacteristic of his eldest daughter. He respected that she was suffering and forced himself not to engage in a battle with her. She was clearly looking for a verbal sparring match in her hurt.

"You know, Dianne was a parishioner at the church, Andrea. Her husband was not but I can probably find her address in the records so you can go and speak to him. Maybe he knows where they ended up. It will be good for Matthew to speak with his father," the Pastor told her. Fire lit up Andrea's hazel eyes and her lips pursed into a thin line. She had told only her father about the woman whom had run off with Philip but she was regretting it at that moment.

"Don't you think if Philip wanted to speak with his son, he would have made an effort in the last month to do that? I am not about to go searching for a man who cares so little about his family that he can't even be bothered to explain himself why he left. Furthermore, do you think Dianne's husband wants to see a reminder of his wife's infidelity on his doorstep? I think the man has had enough to contend with for a while. And please tell me you did not tell Ariel about Philip. I don't want to ruin her wedding."

"I have not said anything to Ariel about Dianne as I promised you. I just came by to see if you needed anything, Andrea. You know I am always here if you want to talk," he told her, putting his hand on her arm comfortingly. Andrea swallowed the lump in her throat. She knew her family meant well but she could not shake the anger she was feeling. She was angry at Philip, at Sam Jameson and at God. She was angry at everyone in her wake, really and anyone who dared speak to her was feeling the brunt of that rage. She opened her mouth to give a snappy retort when the front door flew open and Matthew wandered inside.

"Hi Grandpa!" he called, running over to embrace the older man. Immediately, Andrea choked down her nasty comment and smiled at her son. Matthew was the only one in the world with whom she was not angry. She wondered if that would ever change, if the anger would ever dissipate. She hoped it would. For Matthew's sake and for her own.

Everything Happens For A Reason

"Mom! We have to go!"

Matthew was standing in the foyer, yelling up the stairs. In the bedroom, Andrea stared at herself listlessly in the mirror. She seemed oblivious to how lovely she looked in the long, yellow maid of honor dress that Ariel had chosen. It brought out the gold flecks in her eyes and brought a rosy tint to now pale complexion. She was contemplating skipping the wedding for what seemed like the tenth time that morning and if it weren't for her young son yelling for her, she probably would have crawled back into her bed, fully dressed and gone to sleep. Sighing like it was the last breath she would ever breathe, she wandered down the stairs. At the bottom of the steps, Matthew stood, dressed in a mini tuxedo and for the first time in weeks, Andrea felt her heart well up with intense love for her son. He looked so handsome, his little cumber bun slightly off center, his bow tie on upside down. Guilt flooded her as she realized how unkempt his appearance was, despite his obvious attempt to groom. His hair was far too long, there was sleep in his one eye and toothpaste on his chin. Andrea hurried forward and instinctively licked her thumb to wipe down his face.

"Aw mom!" he cried in protest but Andrea continued to clean him up. Once she had fixed up his suit, she took his arm and they got into the car. Impulsively, she found a popular radio station and blasted it for her son who seemed surprised and happy by her sudden change.

"How are you feeling, mom?" he asked tentatively, partially bopping along to the music. He almost seemed afraid of the answer. Andrea smiled genuinely at him in the rear view mirror.

"I feel like the luckiest woman in the world because I have you as my date," she answered honestly. They arrived at the church in minutes and Ariel looked relieved when her sister appeared in the change room.

"Oh! You're here," she breathed. Andrea was again overwhelmed with shame when she realized that she had almost decided not to come.

"I wouldn't miss your wedding, Ariel," she told her. And as she said it, Andrea realized the words were true. She would not have forsaken her only sister. "You look beautiful."

Ariel smiled at her and turned to the dresser. She picked up a small, square box and handed it to her.

"This is for you," Ariel said. "I hope it helps you to move forward."

Inquisitively, Andrea undid the ribbon and popped off the lid. Inside were two identical keys. Andrea looked up questioningly at her sister.

"Someone is at your house changing the locks right this minute. That way if that pig ever tries to come back, he'll have no way inside." At first, Andrea felt wary but then a flood of happiness swept through her. She felt elated, free by what Ariel had done. She didn't know the entire story but she knew that Andrea was stuck in some depressive limbo and that was her incredibly sweet way of helping her escape. Ariel didn't know it, but a weight lifted off Andrea's chest as she picked up the keys from the velvet box. She rushed over and hugged her sister tightly.

"I love you, Ariel."

"I love you, sis," Ariel whispered, squeezing her back with just as much force.

Outside, the music cued and Ariel wiped away a stray tear and then nodded at Andrea to indicate her readiness. Andrea opened the door leading into the church and started down the aisle, stepping in small even steps. All eyes were trained on her every move. Paul was looking dapper and nervous at the altar, trying to see his bride to be around Andrea's flowing dress. But it wasn't her new brother in law who Andrea's eyes settled upon. Directly to his left was his best man, but beside his best man stood a tall, serious looking man, one of Paul's groomsmen. As she drew closer, a pang of recognition fleeted through her like a bolt but she could not place where she knew him from. The gangly man locked eyes with hers and instantly there was an electric current of surprise and familiarity between the two. It was Christopher. Andrea gasped and went to join her young son at the altar, still staring at the stranger who was bound to her by a cruel fate. She reached down and gently took Matthew's hand, unsure of how to react to her husband's mistress' husband. Then slowly, a shy, warm smile tickled Christopher's lips. For the first time since Philip had abruptly left their lives, everything in the world aligned and felt right again.

AMISH LOVE'S FORGIVENESS

MONICA MANN

December

The service had been lovely as always but Hannah had been unable to concentrate, her mind bustling with dozens of thoughts. As she followed her fiancé's family from the home of one of the member and into the back area of their farm, she wrung her hands nervously.

"Hannah, are you unwell?" She jumped at the sound of Isaac's voice near her ear.

"Not at all! On the contrary, in fact," she replied, peering at him, confusion coloring her face. "What would make you ask such a thing?"

"You seemed not to be paying any attention whatsoever during the sermon. I believe the Bishop scowled at you at one moment." Shocked, Hannah paused in mid step to stare at her husband-to-be, abruptly holding up the line trekking through the field.

"You must be joking!" she cried and then saw the twinkle in Isaac's gentle hazel eyes.

"Perhaps I am but you must admit that your mind has been elsewhere today. What are you thinking about? I noticed the faraway look in your eye from my side of the room!" Hannah laughed and continued toward the barn where the Fisher family had arranged for lunch following their Sunday worship. The winter had been unseasonably warm and Hannah felt somewhat overdressed in her wool cloak. She wished for snow. It did not feel festive without snowflakes gracing the air.

"Well? What is it that plagues your thoughts? Are you reconsidering our marriage?" Again, Isaac's warm eyes lit up with laughter and Hannah grinned broadly at his jesting.

"Certainly not! I am simply concerned about Christmas," Hannah replied, her thoughts beginning to race once more. It was Isaac's turn to show confusion.

"What of Christmas? It is the loveliest time of year. Surely you can't be glum!"

"Not in the least," Hannah replied as they made their way into the spacious structure to join the rest of the congregation. "I am simply worried I have not prepared properly. I have made presents of all of the children and for my parents but I feel as though I have forgotten someone. Which brings me to the Christmas cards. I am always concerned that I have left out a family. Can you imagine how much embarrassment that would bring to us should I omit a single family? What's more is I set up the nativity scene in the front of our home and I cannot find one wise man and two angels. Now I suspect that Rachel has been playing with them but I have yet to find them and she denies knowing their whereabouts. I must have father whittle some for me or else it will be a disaster!"

Suddenly Hannah felt as though a huge weight had been lifted off her shoulders with the confession. Isaac burst into laughter.

"Oh, Hannah! The things which make you fret do amuse me endlessly. It is Christmastime, *liebchen*. It is not a time of worry and fret. That is for the English. We are only to give thanks and spend time with those dearest to us."

"I know, Isaac, but I cannot help wanting Christmas to be perfect! It is my favorite time of the year. And look! This year we haven't even any snow! It hardly seems proper to even set up a tree without the candlelight twinkling off the snow." Hannah pouted but immediately smiled as the truth of his words struck her. Of course he was right; this was not a time of stress. Their way was that of peace and order, not to be overshadowed by the trivialities which the outside word concerned themselves. It was what made the Amish community so special; the ability to block out the unnecessary and focus on the beauty of the basics in life. Hannah could not be happier. She and Isaac had become betrothed in February and their impending marriage was announced to the community in October as per tradition. They had plans to wed the following winter as per tradition and she could not have hoped for a better mate. Despite their engagement, Isaac continued to act as though they were newly enamored with one another, bequeathing her with beautiful flowers and penning poetry for her, words which made her warm to her soul. She was excited to begin her life with him. It seemed that the wedding was millennia away, not merely a year.

"Ah, Hannah, you may worry but your Christmas spirit is infectious," Bishop Philips told her, overhearing the last of their conversation. Blushing scarlet, Hannah turned to acknowledge him, bowing her head.

"Your sermon was well received today, Bishop," Hannah told him, trying to recover from her embarrassment. "It is a rare treat to hear you speak lately. I'm afraid we miss hearing your voice in service. I am pleasantly surprised you have joined us today."

"Unfortunately, I have had business in other districts as of late but I am happy to be back at home. I haven't had the opportunity to congratulate on your betrothal. Isaac, you have done well for yourself. The Yoder family is well respected in our district. Perhaps you will bless them with a son." The Bishop smiled at the couple.

"Not that the Yoder women are any less hard working than any of the men in our community. How is your family? I do not see your father here today," the Bishop continued, looking about, a sudden cloud covering his brown eyes. Hannah and Isaac followed his gaze. Hannah's mother, Ruth stood speaking with several other women while her sisters, Rachel and Miriam ran through the barn, playing a game of tag with some of the other children. As the three continued to look about, Hannah felt a stab of panic in her stomach. It was unheard of for her father, Mark to be absent from church services. She had spent the previous week in Isaac's district at a family member's home. Hannah had been slowly learning the workings of his father's farm at the insistence of Mark who thought it best she understood the complexities of her husband's land as much as possible. As Hannah's cousins resided in close proximity to Isaac's farm, the transition had been seamless and it allowed for their sweet courtship to continue uninterrupted. This also meant, however, that Hannah was not as informed as to the comings and goings of her own family. Brow furrowed, Hannah excused herself and hurried over to her mother, despite Isaac's reactionary hand on her arm to stop her.

"*Mamm*, where is *Daed*?" she whispered in her mother's ear urgently without preamble. Ruth gave Hannah a reproving look and politely exited the conversation in which she was involved.

"Mind your manners, Hannah!" Ruth Yoder chided her daughter.

"I'm sorry Mammi, I am just worried about him. It is unlike him to miss service. I can't recall one instance prior to this one in fact!" Hannah insisted. Seeing her oldest daughter's distress, Ruth's face softened.

"Your father was away at market in Pittsburgh over the weekend. He was expecting to be back last night but the weather turned so he must have been detained. He will likely be home when we return." Hannah exhaled with relief and returned to her fiancé and the Bishop where she reiterated what she had been told. A bell rang to indicate that the meal was about to be served and they all sat at the long tables set up in the middle of building. Yet as they bowed their heads and grace was said, once again, Hannah felt herself distracted by unstoppable thoughts. This time, however, they were not of snowfalls and wise men. Suddenly she her mind was focussed completely on the whereabouts of her father.

"I don't mind, Hannah but I cannot help but feel you are overreacting somewhat," Isaac informed her as they pulled their carriage toward the Yoder farm.

"He is my father. I must know that he is well, Isaac," Hannah replied.

"*Liebchen*, he has been going to market since well before you were born. I am sure he is well. You will see." Isaac smiled boyishly at her and encouraged the horses onward. Hannah felt an uncharacteristic smidgen of annoyance at his placation. She gave him a sidelong look but said nothing. She hoped he was right but some inherent sense told her something was amiss. Inclement weather or not, Mark Yoder would have been at worship. His devotion to God was his priority, probably above his own health and safety. Hannah knew her father. He would have risked riding in a blizzard to honor his commitment to the community. Her mother had arrived back from the Miller farm with Rachel and Miriam and the pale afternoon light was already becoming dark, forsaking dusk altogether.

"I do not see his wagon," Hannah mumbled as they pulled to a stop. Alarm growing in her chest, Hannah recognized the Bishop's carriage which was parked behind the modest house. Hannah did not wait for Isaac to escort her from her seat and instead was running up the front steps to toward the door. As she flew inside the house, she stopped in her tracks. Her mother was on her knees, surrounded by Rachel and Miriam, a look of shock upon their faces. Tears had slipped from their cheeks to the wood floor. Bishop Phillips stood, solemn faced at the base of the stairs, his hat in his hands, his lips pursed into a fine line. They did not need to speak. Hannah already knew.

January

"Hannah, Isaac came calling again," Miriam told her, pushing open the door to the bedroom where her sister sat brushing her long hair, placing it into sections for braiding. Hannah did not respond. Instead she continued to count the strokes, slowly, meticulously smoothing down the strands.

"Hannah? Hannah!" Miriam strode into the room and snatched the utensil from her sister's grip. The older girl looked up in surprise and instinctively grabbed it back.

"What is it?" she demanded, rising to her feet menacingly.

"Isaac was here," Miriam said again. "He would like you to contact him when you are well."

"I am well, thank you. I am simply busy. With *Daed* in the hospital, fighting for his life, someone needs to help *Mamm* run the farm,

Miriam. I cannot up and run off to help him when Isaac has able bodied brothers there. What does he want from me?" Her words were like a torrent of venom and twelve-year-old Miriam stepped back, shocked at her tone.

"I believe that he wants to know if you're well, Hannah. I don't think he wants you to help him on the farm," she offered, timidly, tears filling her eyes. Hannah was immediately contrite but her anger would not lessen.

"Thank you, Miriam. I will be in contact with Isaac shortly." Her sister immediately retreated from the bedroom, closing the door in her wake but Hannah heard her sister's stifled sob before she retreated down the stairs. Hannah knew that her tone had been unreasonably harsh but she could not seem to alleviate the insurmountable rage which had filled her since the horrendous accident her father had endured a mere month before. The driver who had injured Mark so severely on that lone road heading home from the city had yet to be caught and Hannah knew she would not rest until the person had been apprehended and brought to justice. Christmas had come and gone in an unmemorable blur, still filled with family and friends but in a much more somber tone than the joy of the season typically brought. The family had left the candles lit in the windows well after other members of the community had extinguished theirs, a constant flame for others to keep Mark in their prayers. Hannah remembered thinking that the nativity scene was ruined and she had reprimanded Rachel harshly for playing with the wooden characters, reducing the child to a blubbering mess. Much more than that, Hannah could not recall about holiday. There had been an exchange of gifts but Mark's had lay unopened at the hearth and Hannah did not have any recollection of what she had received. Hannah's mother had continued her duty, tending to the farm and caring for the children and Hannah had stepped in to assist as opposed to joining Isaac. At first, Isaac had attempted to stay nearby, offering his unselfish aide to the Yoder family but eventually

Hannah's increasingly sullen behavior had driven him home to his family's land. Still, he had frequently visited his beloved to see how she was faring. More often than not, Hannah made herself unavailable for reasons no one could comprehend. While she never admitted it to anyone, she blamed Isaac also for her father's fate. *If only he had been more vigilante, heeded my words more carefully when I suggested that something was amiss with father,* she told herself time and again. It did not matter that Mark Yoder had been hit on the Saturday night, well before Hannah had any inkling that there was trouble. In Hannah's grief she was beyond reason and all she had remaining was her intense anger. It was irrelevant whom was the recipient of her rage. It needed to be released and Hannah ensured that it was so. Mark's initial prognosis had been grim. The internal damage to his organs was severe and he had several broken bones. He was still on a life support machine in the hospital where he had been taken following being struck. Hannah could not bear to see her strong, vital father in such a condition and had refused to attend his side despite her mother's pleading.

"Hannah, your father needs you there," Ruth had begged her daughter. "Please swallow your repulsion and spend some time at his side. He can hear your prayers."

"He can hear my prayers from here, Mamm. It makes not difference if I am here or there. I cannot bear to see him in such a state with wires poking out of him. Hospitals are filled with harsh lights and harsher people," Hannah countered. "I will not be any good to him there. He knows I am with him in spirit."

Any amount of argument had been futile and eventually Ruth gave up, attending the county hospital with only her two youngest.

"God will not allow him to be taken from us," Ruth assured Hannah one night, attempting to connect with her distraught oldest child.

"God should not have allowed him to have been struck in the first place!" Hannah had yelled back. "God should have been watching out for him. God should have rendered the driver comatose and on life support!"

There was no point in debating the issue. In her mind, Hannah would not rest until she saw the face of the person responsible for the atrocity writhing in shame, guilt and agony.

<u>February</u>

"Ma'am I understand your anger but there we are doing everything we can."

Hannah's blue eyes flashed but she checked her temper.

"Sir, it has been almost three months and you have absolutely no leads regarding the driver of the vehicle which struck my father. Surely you should be exploring other avenues to catch this animal! Doesn't it concern you that this kind of person is driving on your streets where your children walk?"

"Hannah!" Isaac gently placed his hand on her shoulder as she rose from her chair to confront the police detective at the desk. He turned apologetically to the detective.

"Hannah has been under a lot of stress since the accident," Isaac told the man who nodded understandingly.

"Of course, we fully get that and we sympathize," Detective Adams replied. "I have heard that your father is no longer on life support. We are all very happy to hear that."

Hannah felt her hands clench into fists, her nails digging into her palms.

"Yes, praise the Lord for small favors," she answered shortly, her eyes narrowing, ignoring Isaac's fingers which were now increasing pressure on her shoulder. "However, that does not change anything. Is this why nothing has been done to find the monster responsible? Because he is alive? Next time he may not be so lucky if this person is still on the road!"

"Miss Yoder, I assure you that we are doing everything we can but it is very difficult with the circumstances. There were no witnesses, it was a dark road..."

Hannah threw up her hands. She understood. Mark Yoder was not a priority to these people. He would have to be dead or English for them to care. They were just going to say words until she left them alone. Worried she would not be able to contain a barrage of words threatening to escape her lips, she turned to leave without responding. Hannah heard Isaac apologizing for her rudeness once more but Hannah did not wait for her fiancé. Moments later, he was at her side, breathing heavily from chasing her down the crowded street. Under normal circumstances, Hannah would have been unnerved by the throng of people in her midst. It was not like her to visit town, much preferring the quiet way of her community but it had been months and there had been no advancement regarding the driver who had struck her father. Against her mother's pleas, Hannah had taken it upon herself to meet with the detective face-to-face.

"Please, Hannah, Bishop Phillips has been in constant contact with the police. You must not go and bother them."

"If not me, then who?" Hannah had demanded.

"Go see your father! He needs you!" Ruth implored. But the words had fallen upon deaf ears and Ruth had summoned Isaac to accompany her now wayward daughter into town. Isaac had appeared as Hannah was setting off.

"Hannah! That was rude!" He breathed, struggling to keep up with her brisk stride.

"Well perhaps that's what they need, rudeness. Niceties don't seem to be getting us anywhere."

"Hannah, I'm sure they are doing everything they can – "

"It is not enough!" Hannah snapped. Isaac stopped walking, taken aback by her tone. Hannah had never had occasion to speak to him in such a manner. He watched after the woman he was destined to marry and he wondered what had happened to the gentle, even tempered girl he had courted. He understood she was frazzled, not acting rationally but deep down, he hoped that girl was not lost forever.

March

"Hannah, you have not been at worship in several weeks."

The statement was blunt but not filled with accusation. Bishop Phillips simply stared at her, his brown eyes wise with understanding. She shrugged nonchalantly and did not turn from the hens from which she was collecting eggs.

"God knows where I am," she responded flippantly. Bishop Phillips drew closer to her inside the coop, ignoring the squawking of the animals in his midst.

"It is not simply of God knowing where to find you," he told her, gently. "Worship is a place of community, a place where others can shoulder your burden while asking for the Lord's help."

Hannah reeled around to glare at him.

"What does the community know of shouldering my burden?" she asked. "Can they find the animal who ran down my father like a rabid dog in the street? Have they made him pay penance for the harm he has caused my family?"

A warm, fatherly hand reached her shoulder and the Bishop smiled weakly.

"Perhaps not, child, but your suffering is our suffering also. We grow together and we will support one another. That is what makes us strong. You cannot fight this burden alone."

"I am not alone," Hannah retorted. "I have my family. I have Isaac."

But even as she said the words, Hannah tried to remember the last time she had spent more than a few moments with her betrothed. She could not. She shoved the thought from her mind. It did not matter. The only importance was figuring out who had hurt her father. Isaac would have to understand that her priority was with her father.

April

"Hannah! Hannah!"

Miriam and Rachel's footsteps could be heard reverberating through her bedroom well before the door flew open and the twins appeared. Her heart in her throat, Hannah turned away from the window out of which she had been staring for well over an hour, lost in thought.

"What is it? Is it *Daed*? Is he dead?"

Shocked, the girls recoiled at her words, smiles fading from their lips.

"No!" Rachel cried. "Of course not! Why would you say such a thing?"

In truth, Hannah had been waiting for news of the like and had been since the day he had been hospitalized. Her heart began to slow and she forced herself to smile at her sisters.

"I'm sorry. What is it?"

"He's awake! *Daed* is awake!"

Hannah's slowing pulse picked up speed once more. She flung herself into her siblings' arms and the three rejoiced at the news.

"He is? When did this happen? What did the doctors say?" Hannah whipped the questions at them rapid fire. Ruth appeared in the doorway. Her face was gaunt from exhaustion and emotion.

"He will still need some time to recover in the hospital," Ruth answered. "But his ribs are healing as well as his kidneys." Hannah pulled away from the twins and looked at her mother, her face alight with excitement. *Now we will catch you! Daed will identify the driver and it will all be over!*

"Did he say anything?" she pressed. "Can he identify the driver? Or the vehicle? Does he know who hit him?"

Ruth's sky colored eyes clouded over and she regarded her daughter for a moment.

"Hannah, it is not healthy for you to focus so direly on the driver. God will sort out what to do with him. You must instead think of your father and concentrate on good thoughts." Hannah scowled at her mother.

"I am focussed on *Daed*! That is why I want to find out who did this to him! Why am I met with resistance at every turn? You, Isaac, Bishop Phillips. Am I the only one who cares about seeing justice served?"

Ruth pursed her lips together and did not reply. Hannah continued to stare at her mother.

"Well? What did he say? Did he identify the man or not?" she demanded. Ruth sighed heavily.

"No, Hannah. He cannot speak. He had a stroke."

May

Springtime held the promise of new birth for everyone in the community but Hannah. She found herself tending to chores indoor more and more. Isaac had ceased visiting altogether and Hannah found herself in the police station once a week, hounding Detective Adams mercilessly. Where the women in the community would have typically begun to make suggestions for her wedding, offering assistance and chattering cheerfully of their own nuptials, Hannah found herself almost isolated, something she was quite content in discovering. The feeling of helplessness which had overwhelmed her was becoming a suffocating blanket as more time passed and left her no closer to finding the heathen who had hurt her father. She still had not gone to the hospital to see Mark, despite reports from her family that he was faring quite well. He still had not managed to recoup his motor skills and Hannah did not want the face of a crippled man plaguing her already dark thoughts. She would not rest until someone had paid.

June

"You are attending service."

Her voice was flat and left no room for argument. Hannah opened her mouth to speak but caught the anger in her mother's usually gentle eyes and thought better of voicing her thoughts. Grudgingly, she retreated to her room to ready herself for worship.

The family hosting church services was a neighbor and the Yoder family arrived just as Bishop Phillips rose to speak. He fixated his eyes upon Hannah and began to preach of forgiveness. Hannah closed her ears and averted her eyes. *I will forgive when the driver asks for forgiveness. Not one moment before. And even then, I may not.*

July

He came home on a Tuesday and several members of the community were present to welcome Mark. They brought flowers and honey and bombarded him and the family with well wishes. Isaac and his family had driven in also but Hannah only watched the event from her bedroom window, unable to watch her enfeebled father slowly stumble his way up the steps of the veranda. Her eyes filled with tears but whether they were of guilt or pain, she was not sure. As Mark made his way inside with the help of his wife and two youngest daughters, Isaac lifted his eyes toward Hannah's bedroom window. His own eyes were filled with sadness and Hannah quickly ducked back behind the curtains, not willing to look at him. It had been a long while since they had spent time together and she admitted that she missed his company dearly. She often wondered what he was doing and if he thought of her. The look on his face told Hannah that he did long for her as she did him. Swallowing the urge to run downstairs and beg him for forgiveness, Hannah sat on the edge of the bed. She wondered if anything would ever be the same again.

August

"Hannah! Hannah!"

Rachel almost knocked Hannah over as she barreled into the barn. Hannah looked up at her quickly.

"What is it?"

"*Daed* said his first clear word!" Hannah felt hope swell in her chest.

"What did he say?" she asked, wiping her hands on her apron and following Rachel out of the building, toward the house.

"He said 'Hannah.' He's asking for you!"

<u>September</u>

Progress was swift from that moment onward. Every day, Mark Yoder began to say more. He was required to see a specialist in town to assist him in his walking but Hannah was beginning to see signs of the same, strapping man she had admired her whole life. She found it less painful to be in his presence but she still could not help but feel enraged at his condition. When Hannah did stay at his side, she pressed him for details of the accident. To her relief, he recalled a great deal and Hannah feverishly wrote down the details as Mark remembered, every day adding more to the description. Finally, after three weeks, she had a proper sketch of the vehicle and possibly the driver which she immediately took to the police station. *Now we've got you!* She thought smugly.

<u>October</u>

"Are we still to marry?"

The question startled Hannah as she had not heard Isaac at her back. He had been watching her from the porch as she hummed to herself, picking wildflowers. Oddly, the upcoming wedding had been fresh in her mind for the first time in months. Since delivering the description to the police, Hannah had felt as though they were nearing absolution and a giant weight seemed to have been lifted from her shoulders. She stared in surprise at her fiancé.

"I certainly hope so, Isaac. Are you reconsidering?" She felt faint as she waited for him to answer. Slowly, Isaac made his way down the steps and toward his betrothed.

"I feel as though we have become very distant these past months, Hannah. I wondered if you still wished for us to marry." She met the distance between them and offered him her hands.

"Forgive me, Isaac! I have been consumed with worry for my father. Of course I have never thought for a moment that you and I would not be wed." Isaac eagerly accepted her hands and squeezed them gently, smiling with relief.

"I am glad you have finally decided to forgive and move on," he told her. "I knew the sensible woman I know was in there somewhere."

Hannah beamed back at him.

"It will be very easy to move on once this man is caught! I believe the police will finally catch him now!"

The smile died on Isaac's lips as he stared at Hannah. He realized that she was still consumed with the idea of catching the driver. Wisely, he said nothing but a sense of unease filled his stomach. Would this never end?

<u>November</u>

"You must be very excited with the upcoming wedding, Hannah. It has been quite a year for you and your family. It will be a relief to have cause for celebration over bad times, I would say," Bishop Phillips said after service. Hannah smiled widely and nodded, glancing at Isaac. He smiled meekly.

"Yes, we are looking forward to it. A Christmas wedding may seem a bit ostentatious but it is my favorite time of year and Isaac has been kind enough to indulge my whimsy on this matter," Hannah answered happily.

"Well I think it is a wonderful idea. It will only solidify your union with Christ. I am happy to see your father up and about."

"Yes, he is already back into manning the farm as he was prior to the accident."

"Well that is wonderful news, Hannah. It must certainly alleviate your desire to see the perpetrator arrested. It was not good for you to be so fixated on such negative thoughts for so long," the Bishop told her, turning to nod at other members of the congregation.

"No, Bishop, I can focus on other things now. The police are closing in on the animal now that my father has given them somewhere to look. We will have our justice in due time. I must leave it in their hands now." The Bishop looked at Hannah sharply.

"Your father knows who hit him?"

"He gave a very accurate description of the man, yes," Hannah replied. "But as you say, Bishop, it is in God's hands now. I have decided to focus more on my husband-to-be and deal with the criminal when he is found."

Bishop Phillips nodded, his eyes dark.

"Yes, it is in God's hands," he agreed.

December

The police were standing on her porch and Hannah felt her heart leap into her throat.

"Miss Yoder? Is your father home?" the detective asked her, peering over her shoulder. She nodded eagerly and granted them entry. Mark sat in a rocking chair in the front room. He rose to his feet with an agility he did not possess even two weeks prior.

"Please do come in, officers," he told them, cordially. Awkwardly, the detectives ventured into the humble home and stood in the doorway.

"Have you found the man responsible?" Hannah demanded. "Is that why you're here?"

Mark gave her a reproachful look.

"Hannah, where are your manners? Would you like a beverage?" Both men shook their heads and fidgeted nervously.

"Well?" Hannah demanded when there was silence. "Have you news?"

"Hannah!" Mark chided again but the lead detective held up his hand and nodded.

"Yes, Miss Yoder. We have your man. Someone has turned himself in."

Hannah's face went through a variety of changes; hope, shock and then anger.

"He turned himself in?" she almost yelled. "After one year? What kind of monster lets a family suffer for an entire year before confessing his crime?"

"Hannah…"

"Yes, Miss Yoder but frankly, in these situations, it is extremely difficult to find hit and run drivers. We are very lucky that someone did come forward at all," the policeman interjected. "But I do understand your frustration."

"I doubt it," Hannah mumbled. "Where is he?"

"He is in the county lock up. We would like your father to come with us to see if he can be identified in a line up but he had fully confessed to the accident."

"Who is he? A young, drunk English boy?" Hannah asked contemptuously, already envisioning the short haired punk, smoking a marijuana cigarette. Again, an uncomfortable silence ensued. Hannah stared at the men expectantly.

"Who is he?"

Detective Adams cleared his throat.

"It is someone you know," he said evasively. Hannah exchanged concerned looks with her father.

"Who?" she pressed.

"He is your Bishop. Daniel Phillips."

"Hello Hannah."

Hannah felt her legs turn to jelly as she stared at her much-loved Bishop behind the bars of the county jail.

"It is true," she whispered. "How did this happen?"

"I wish I could explain it to you, child but there is nothing I can say which will take away what you and your family have endured over this year."

"Please tell me what happened," she begged, her eyes filled with tears. The Bishop took a breath and told her the story he had relived in his head over and over since the day it had happened.

He had travelled the road hundreds, if not thousands of times before but Bishop Phillips had not slept more than two hours a night in over three weeks. There had been minor unrest in two of the neighboring districts, some petty squabbling which should have resolved itself but somehow a miniscule issue had become a weeks long debate. He was grateful that he was finally able to return home to his district. The car in which he rode had been a gift from a Bishop in one of the districts who had taken pity upon his constant state of commute. Bishop Phillips had to admit that it was more luxurious than his hard riding horse and cart but he also knew that he should not get too attached.

As the headlights lit the way around the road, his heart leapt into his throat. A doe stood frozen in the road, shocked by the onset. In his exhaustion, it took a few seconds for his reaction time to match up with his vision. He slammed on the brakes and veered to the left of the road, barely grazing the tail of the animal but full on impacting something else; a horse drawn cart. The mare whinnied in pain and shock as the Bishop struggled to steady the still moving vehicle. As all was still, Bishop Phillips opened the door to the car and ran toward the now toppled buggy. Inside lay the still body of Mark Yoder, seemingly lifeless. Bishop Phillips stood stock still, unsure of what to do. I must stay and wait for help, he told himself. Then he remembered the two glasses of wine he had consumed with supper. Slowly, he backed up and slipped back into the car, driving away undetected into the black night.

Tears fell from her lids onto her cheeks as she looked at the broken man before her. She thought of how badly she had wanted him to suffer but all she could think of was how much he had already suffered. He must have wanted to ease her agony a thousand times but had been trapped in his own nightmare.

"I understand that you must loathe me, Hannah. You have every right to feel as such," Bishop Phillips told her, his voice cracking. Gently, Hannah reached between the bars and offered the Bishop her hands. He grabbed them instantly and looked at her pleadingly.

"I forgive you," she said simply.

Christmas

"Oh, Hannah you look beautiful," Ruth told her daughter, embracing her warmly. "I have been looking forward to this for so long!"

Hannah laughed.

"Yes, me too Mammi," she joked and lovingly returned her mother's caress. She looked at herself in the mirror one last time. She vowed to her reflection that with this new start she would forsake all anger and rely on God to give her strength in the worst of times. She knew how fortunate she was that Isaac had been strong enough to stand by her during such a trying time and she would never forget it. She turned and looked at her mother and sisters.

"Are you ready?" Miriam asked, hopping back and forth from one foot to another. Hannah looked around and suddenly her stomach dropped.

"Where is *Daed*?" she asked, feeling a familiar sense of panic seize her. The curtain was quickly drawn and Mark strolled in, his gait strong and perfect.

"I am here, *liebchen*. Do you think I would miss giving away my oldest daughter?" he answered. His voice was slightly slower than it had been but his words were perfectly pronounced. There was no sign of the stroke he had suffered. Hannah exhaled. Everything was right again.

DEEP IN THE AMISH HEART

MEGHAN MASON

Sarah's day began as any other. The sky was clear and blue with a scattering of pillow clouds, and Sarah was walking the two mile stretch between her home and her father's general store in town. Each morning she had to arise from her sleep before sunrise to fulfill all the household duties. There were chickens to be fed, produce to be picked, and breakfast to be prepared for herself, her daed, Jacob, and her two younger siblings. Sarah was the oldest, at seventeen, then came her schwester Hope at nine years old, and finally boppli bruder, Noah. Their maam had passed away during childbirth just a year ago next month. Noah had not even had his first birthday yet. In Amish life, this meant that Sarah, being the eldest daughter, was now responsible for keeping house and raising her younger siblings. It was an enormous responsibility, but one that Sarah did with a willing and loving heart. She loved to sing softly to herself as she dressed in her pale blue dress, white apron and bonnet. As she completed all the morning chores, Sarah liked to sing her favorite church hymns. It helped to make the chores go by faster, and always served to put her in a good mood.

Today, as Sarah made her way down the dirt path that led to town, she hummed a little tune, and thought about what a long day it would be for her working at her daed's store. She loved her father, but Jacob Williams was renowned in the small Amish community as a very strict task master. He could certainly be overbearing at times, but Sarah understood how difficult life had become for him since her mamm's death. Jacob had loved his wife, Elizabeth very much. They had married at only sixteen years old, and planned on making a life together as they grew in their love for one another into ripe old age. It was not Gott's will however, and now the Williams family had to adjust to life without mamm. Sarah knew her daed was lonely most times, and that that was what made him so domineering at times. It didn't make things any easier on Sarah, however, and taking care of the home, plus working at the store was exhausting. She did this all without complaint, and thanked Gott for her many blessings. The store sold local goods from the community farmers, and some of the women sewed items of clothing or household linens upon special request. Often, specific Englischers would place orders for tablecloths or various linens, and the ladies who had grown children, thus having extra time on their hands, would take up the task.

Sarah entered the store, and greeted her father in traditional Pennsylvania Dutch, as he was of the Old Order who still adhered strictly to Amish customs, "Guder Mariye, daed," she said cheerfully. As per usual, Jacob eyed his eldest daughter with a certain unfounded suspicion, but returned her morning greeting just the same.

"Sarah, there is much to accomplish today. You can start with sweeping and dusting the shelves, and then take over the accounts book. I need to go to see Farmer Pickens about eggs, since he is late with delivery," he stated. This was bound to be a long day, but if she was left alone in the store for most of the day, she could at least indulge herself in singing. Daed did not approve of Sarah's love of song outside of the religious environment or outside the home, as was the custom of her faith. Nonetheless, Sarah felt it to be a harmless enough past time if she wasn't running around town singing for everyone to hear. Jacob watched her as she retrieved the broom, and then he departed for Farmer Pickens'.

As Sarah swept the already very clean oak floors, she sang a lovely hymn from last Sunday's service. It was called, "The Lord Provides," and she loved it because of the sweet notes and fortifying lyrics. She was alone in the store, and she allowed herself to really sing out. Singing was the thing that made her feel the happiest, and soon enough she was in a world of her own.

Outside, a young man strolled along the road, thinking about how relieved he felt about having made the move to a simpler life in the country. He enjoyed the pristine air, and the beautiful woods, and had a healthy respect for the Amish community. The outlying farms and cottages that were not Amish, coexisted peacefully together, respecting one another's privacy and traditions. The town called Havensville was a perfect place to call home after the disaster he had left behind him in the big city of Pittsburgh. The young man was just eighteen, but mature enough to recognize the dysfunction of his family life. His father's alcoholism had been taking its toll on him and his mother for many years, and she had recently passed away from a lengthy battle with cancer. He tried to care for his father, but he would have none of it, and continued his wayward lifestyle. So, after much thought, he decided to leave school, where he was studying music, and start fresh somewhere new. The young man packed his bags, gathered what meager funds he had saved from after school jobs, and caught the next bus out to the countryside. He stopped short when he saw the quaint wooden store in front of him. It was painted a fresh white with simple blue trim, and had a small garden of wildflowers in the front. There was a cobblestone walkway leading up to the entry, and a hanging sign above the door that read, "William's General Store." Nothing flashy, but it was adorned with a little bluebird in the righthand corner of the square sign. The store looked like something out of a storybook with its flowers and front porch swing. He decided he should go in and stock up on supplies and grocery items since this was his very first day in town. He entered the store, and there he observed a modest, yet beautiful young woman singing her heart out as she dusted the many shelves behind the register. Her back was turned to him, and she had not noticed the bell as he had entered the store.

"Excuse me please, miss?"

Sarah gave a startled jump, as she whipped around. She felt embarrassed that she hadn't heard anyone enter the store, and here she was singing away!

"Oh, my goodness! I'm terribly sorry. I didn't hear you come in, sir," Sarah replied.

"It is not a problem. I quite enjoyed your song. You have a lovely singing voice," the young man said. Sarah blushed crimson at his compliment, as she was shy towards strangers, and she had not seen this young man around the village area,

"How may I help you, Mr....." Sarah inquired.

"I am hardly worthy of the title of Mr., but my name is John Anders, and I have only just arrived here in Havensville this early morning," He replied. Sarah thought him a fine-looking man, around her own age, but wondered why on earth he had come here to live in such a small and isolated place, "Where are you coming from, Mr. Anders? And you are with your family, I presume?"

"No, I am here alone from Pittsburgh. It was time for me to start a new life of my own. This place seemed good enough as any other, I guess," offered John, "and please, call me John, and may I ask your name?"

"Ok, my name is Sarah, and my father owns the store. Alright then, John, what would you like?" Sarah began to list what sundries and groceries the simple store offered, but John stopped her, and said he was here for basic living supplies, like food and a few other items such as general toiletries,

"Miss Sarah, I guess I would be grateful if you just took charge and filled my basket with whatever cooking things you think best, and I'll go in search of my personal items?" said John hopefully, as he was not at all knowledgeable about what exactly he would need.

As Sarah made up a large basket of fruits, vegetables, and other things she thought necessary for a young bachelor, John returned to the counter with another basket filled with such items as a hairbrush, toothbrush, toothpaste, sponges, and other assorted things. John thought Sarah was delightful, friendly and kind, and decided to ask her a few questions about Havensville,

"Sarah, thank you for helping me sort out all these things! You are such a help, because this is honestly the first time I have ever been out on my own, and I haven't the slightest clue what I'm planning to do. I do not even have anywhere to stay yet, or any prospects of a job. Do you happen to know of anywhere that may offer a room, and perhaps some honest work?"

Sarah studied John, and figured since he had a gentle looking face and good manners, that she really should help welcome the new comer to his new home. She thought hard for a moment or two, and then replied,

"I know Farmer Pickens has been late with his egg deliveries lately, now that his Betty has had their boppli, oh! I mean baby..." she stammered, remembering that John was likely unfamiliar with their ways of speaking, but without skipping a beat, John said,

"No, please Sarah, use your traditional words. I took the liberty of reading up on Amish tradition and life during the bus ride. I am proud to say that I think I now am familiar with many unfamiliar words!" Sarah was surprised at John's eagerness and willingness to learn some Pennsylvania Dutch, and this only made him more attractive in her eyes.

"Anyways, John, I was going to say that Farmer Pickens might have some dairy work for you, and my daed may like to have a helper with building the new barn at home. He's out at Pickens place, now, but should be returning within the hour," Sarah volunteered. For am Englischer, John Anders was certainly a nice young man, and she was impressed with his independence and desire to fit into the small community.

John smiled, as he paid for his groceries, while Sarah bagged them in plain paper sacks. He was going to have his hands full with these many bags, but he could make it to wherever he was going just fine. He just had to figure out just where it was he was going, and he decided to engage Sarah in more conversation, "Well, perhaps I should wait outside then for your father to return, so that I can sort out some work. I have nowhere in particular to go just now, so I guess your front porch swing is as good a place as any to pass the time." His simple manner made Sarah smile again, and she said he was welcome to the swing while she finished up her duties inside.

"Perhaps you would care for some homemade lemonade when I am finished?" Sarah offered.

"Yes, that sounds wonderful, Sarah. Thank you, kindly! Will you join me then, once you're finished?" he asked hopefully. Again, Sarah blushed, but she did agree to sit awhile on the swing until her father returned, if no other customer came calling. John went outside, and Sarah hurriedly went back to her dusting.

Once outside, John scanned the pretty little porch, and sat down on the swing. It was of fine craftsmanship, and constructed from a sturdy pine, he thought. He sat there quietly thinking that he had made an excellent choice in coming to this place. If everyone was as nice as Sarah Williams, then he was sure to feel at home. Now he just had to find a place to live. He felt a bit nervous, since it was approaching afternoon, and he did not want to be homeless on his first night in a new town. As John was busy fretting about what to do next, Sarah had finished her work, and was preparing a tray of iced cold lemonade. She thought he might be hungry after his long bus journey, and so she made up a plate of sandwiches and sliced some fresh peaches from her own orchard. She had brought them as part of her own midday meal, but felt it would be nice to share with John. She liked the idea of sitting out front with the young man, even though father would probably not approve of her sitting alone with a stranger. She carried the tray outside, and noticed the look of obvious concern on John's face.

"Whatever is the matter, John?" as she placed the lunch things on the side table. John looked thankfully at her, and said,

"Sarah, you certainly did not have to go to such trouble on my account! Thank you. I do feel hungry. To tell you the truth, I am concerned about where I might find lodging for tonight. I am sure I can find something more permanent as I become more familiar with the folks in town," John confided.

"Don't you worry just yet," she reassured him, and poured him a nice glass of lemonade. She placed a sandwich in his lap, and began to make pleasant conversation about the weather, and who was who in town, and so on...John couldn't help but recall her beautiful singing voice when he had first entered the store. She had such a lovely voice! He could think of nothing more wonderful than to hear her singing again, as he missed his music studies, and was a decent singer himself, but he knew he must not seem to forward. He hoped he might someday hear her angelic voice again, as he got to know her better, and realized he was lost in his daydreams of her, as she chattered on. He forced himself back to reality, and listened to everything she was saying regarding life in and around the town. The care she had taken making him sandwiches and sharing the juicy peaches did not go unnoticed. He could not have wished for a lovelier welcome.

Just after a half hour or so, Jacob's horse drawn buggy was making its way towards the store front. Sarah could already see his tense looking eyes, and frowny expression, as he noted that his daughter was sitting unattended with a strange young newcomer. He parked the buggy hastily, and walked briskly up the front steps to the swing,

"What have we here, Sarah? Why are you not minding the store?" he demanded.

"Daed, please welcome Mr. John Anders from Pittsburgh. He has travelled here by bus to make a life for himself, and came in to purchase his necessities," announced his daughter. Jacob stared at the young Englischer with some uneasiness, as he was always wary of outsiders. You never knew how they would take to the Amish customs, after all. Nonetheless, Jacob was not to be a rude man, so he extended his hand in greeting,

"Kannscht du Pennsilfaanisch Deitsch schetzer?" blurted Jacob, knowing full well that Mr. Anders certainly did not speak Pennsylvania Dutch. It was Jacob's way of distancing himself from the young stranger, and he was obviously annoyed that Sarah had engaged him in conversation, and then apparently fed him as well! A little too welcoming, he thought to himself.

"Uh, no, I think what you said was 'Do I speak Pennsylvania Dutch? I confess I am not very familiar with it as of yet, but did have a chance to study some on my way here. I am a quick study, luckily, and hope to pick up the language here and there," John returned quickly. He could understand a father's protective nature, and realized he was the new person in town, so he had better do his best to make a proper first impression,

"It is good to meet you, Mr. Williams," said John, and then Sarah thankfully took over and explained that he was in search of some steady work, and a place to cover his head.

Jacob's predictable answer to this announcement was, "Englischers! Sie scheie sich vun haddiArewat." John made out at least some of what was said, and promptly and wisely replied, "No sir, I am a hard worker, and am willing to take on anything that is available. I need to learn to make my own way in the world now that I am my own man. I can assure you I am a man of my word, and an honest worker for anyone who needs help. I studied music, but am not afraid of a man's work in the fields or building. Whatever needs to be done, I will do it, and I will do it well," promised John Anders. Jacob had to admit that he approved of the boy's answer, though he was no boy, but rather a young man of about eighteen to twenty years of age. As much as he would have preferred otherwise, Jacob knew he needed help building the barn that was to house the new horses, goats, and cows. They were due in for delivery from the neighboring town of Lancaster in three weeks' time, and he would never finish the job alone,

"Tell you what, young Mr. Anders. I need a strong young man to build my barn with me. I'll need ya to be schmaert (smart) and no schlofkopp (sleepyhead)! I'll give ya board in the shack out back. Sarah will make it home for ya, and put some extra furnishings in there. It'll be small, but I imagine it's a darn sight better than nothing.," and as Jacob had finished his little speech and offer of work and board, John couldn't help but smile wide! This was just perfect, and exactly what he needed, which was not much. Just somewhere to call home, and a place where he could lay his head at night after a hard day's work, "Many thanks, sir! I am much obliged to you for your kind and generous offer." Sarah could only stare blankly at her father's unexpected good nature, and she couldn't help but feel a surge of excitement that John, whom she now considered a friend, would be staying right there on their farm! It would no doubt mean one more mouth to cook and clean for, but she was happy to have the friendly John join her little clan. She enjoyed her household duties, and one more surely would not be any bother.

Jacob said, "Mr. Anders, you wait here till closing time, and we'll go home in the buggy, and get you situated. Sarah, you will have extra work tonight getting Mr. Anders settled and preparing the meal. I expect a satisfying meal, so go on home and get started early then! No time to be standing around on the porch making idle talk," and so he dismissed Sarah, and off she went back home to give that shack a thorough cleaning. By now, Hope would be home from her book learning, and together they could muster what strength they had, and drag some extra furnishings into John's new home. It would take some effort to make that old shack into a home, but she would do it happily for John.

As evening fell, Sarah and Hope had just put the finishing touches on John's new abode, when the buggy arrived. The two men got out, and she noticed that John had not cases or trunk. That meant he had only the clothes on his back! She would start to sewing him some pants and shirts just as soon as she could. But now, there was a beef stew to get on the table for supper, and children to wash up. She practically ran back to the house to check on her stew, and slice the bread. Her father would want dinner on the table straight away.

"Welcome to our home," said Sarah, and she introduced him to each member of the family, including boppli, Noah, and then served up the stew. Everyone enjoyed pleasant conversation, though Jacob kept fairly quiet. He was not one for conversation. Sarah noticed that John ate his supper and hoped that he had had enough to eat. She offered homemade apple tart for dessert, "Sarah, I must thank you for your family's hospitality. I must admit I heard you singing earlier this afternoon in the store! You have an exceptional voice, if you don't mind my saying so. Do you sing at church service? You should not deprive the rest of the town of such a heavenly sound. Do you think you'll sing at the Town Square Picnic your father was telling me about on the way home?" Jacob let his fork drop with a clatter, and John suspected he had somehow misspoke,

"I will have you know, Mr. Anders, that we Amish do not sing for personal glory. Sarah will sing at service only; do you hear that maedel!" spat her father. Sarah already knew how her father felt about her love for singing, and couldn't help but feel sorry for the way John must feel at her father's reproach. Sarah nodded in agreement, and quietly resumed eating her apple tart. When dinner was finished, she cleared the table, and washed up the dishes. Meanwhile, Jacob had taken John out to survey the barn building, and explain what was needed in the coming three weeks. It was going to be a stretch, thought John, to get that barn built in time for the animals, but a promise was a promise. He'd get the job done mostly on his own while Jacob was working at the store. Then they would work on it together till dark in the weeks to come.

John made his way to his meager home, but upon entering the front door, he was amazed at what a spectacular job Sarah had done sprucing the place up! The wooden floors gleamed and smelled like fresh soap, and she had put pretty little curtains up around the window. He felt badly that she had been put to such trouble dragging in furniture, but was relieved to see it was just a simple chair and table, a cot made up into a comfy looking bed. She had supplied him with lots of fluffy blankets and a pillow, and there was a plain white porcelain ewer and basin for washing. It was perfect! Simple and comfortable was all he wanted or needed. He felt a strange stirring in his heart that Sarah was the one who had taken such care in setting up his new home. He definitely liked her very much, and looked forward to seeing her at meal times and whenever else he could squeeze in a moment with her. He wondered what she thought of him, and the sound of her singing filled his head as he fell asleep that night.

The next few days passed by with plenty of work on the barn. In fact, Sarah and the others only saw the menfolk at meals. She had to admit to herself that she missed talking with John. Her father retired earlier than normal that night directly after supper, and John was nice enough to help wash up. She offered him a hot cup of rose-hip tea by the fireside, as she readied Hope and Noah for bedtime. With the younger ones fast asleep, she joined John in the main room. She had been softly singing a good night song for the children, and he had listened with great joy from his chair by the fire,

"Sarah, I wanted to say thank you for making me so at home. I love being here, and sharing life with your family. Sure, your father may be a bit brusque, but he means well, and is very protective of you as a father should be. I couldn't help but overhear your singing the children to sleep. It was very beautiful. I would be honored to come to service to hear you sing if I may? Am I allowed as an outsider to attend?" he inquired.

"Yes, John, all are welcome. You will be seated on one side, along with all the other single men. You will fit in, because they do not yet have beards. Those are for the married men only," she giggled slightly as she imagined John taking part in the Amish service. It rotated from house to house every Sunday, "My father will like that you are wanting to attend our service. He will be impressed, and I already know that he values all your arduous work. He told me so just yesterday morning as he left for the general store," confided Sarah. John had been working double time to make certain that the barn would be ready on time. He also hoped Mr. Williams might need him to care for the animals, since he was responsible for tending the store. John would like to stay on, sharing in their lives, and he would be willing to learn how to tend to the animals and any farm work for her father. It was getting late, and John stood to make his way across the yard to his room. "Sarah," he asked nervously, "Would it be appropriate for you to walk with me to the shack?"

"Well, father is asleep, so I do not see any problem with that," she agreed tentatively. She had grown to really admire John, and hoped he would stay on and perhaps be happy here. But, she knew that he was an Englischer, and would always remain an outsider. She also knew that she could never entertain the idea of him courting her, as she was expected to court an Amish man. It was time for her to be looking for her own husband, as she was of age, and this was the Amish tradition. She put the thought out of her mind, and got up to walk John back to his tiny home.

As they walked together, John looked up at the starry sky, and commented on the cool night, "Are you warm enough, Sarah? If not, please take my coat," as he noticed her shiver in the moonlight. He loved the way she always blushed in his presence. He hoped that Sarah felt for him as much as he felt for her. For he was already falling in love with her, but knew he must tread very carefully, in order to keep Jacob a happy and trusting man.

"Would you sing a hymn for me, Sarah?" asked John, as he looked at her by the starlight, "It is allowed if it is a hymn, honoring Gott, as you say," and they grinned at his use of the Amish expression.

"I guess it would be ok," she said, and she chose the very same song that she had been singing that day he entered the general store. John listened to every lilt of her voice, and suppressed his urge to kiss her. That would have been too soon, and he was determined to make no gestures that she may not expect, though he sensed she might be hoping for the same thing. However, there was the issue of John not being part of the Amish faith, and this was going to present a huge problem if he were to act upon his feelings. He couldn't help but take her hand in his as they reached his door. Sarah stopped her song rather abruptly, and shied away from John immediately. He felt he had blundered the moment, but she did not run off,

"I am sorry to make you uncomfortable, Sarah. It's just that you sing so beautifully and sweetly, that it fills my heart with such happiness. I understand that I am not of your faith, but there is something I must speak to your father about before the end of the month. I am considering joining the Amish in life and in faith. I want to be worthy of your affections, as you must have guessed by now, my dear little songbird. I cannot bear not to hear your lovely singing. It is too bad that the Amish do not allow singing for secular purposes, but I can understand why."

Sarah stood somewhat aghast at John's admission of love, though she returned his feelings wholeheartedly. She would like nothing so much in this world as to be able to love John, but there were obvious hurdles that would have to be addressed, "John, it is very uncommon for an outsider to join the Amish ways, but it is not unheard of. We have never had one in our small community, but I have heard tale of it in larger ones," she stated confidently. Did she dare allow herself to love him back? This was a question that would have to wait. They said their good nights, and John watched as she got to her front door safely. John was more than a little intimidated at the thought of having to discuss becoming Amish with Jacob. He resolved to have that conversation before this Sunday. With that settled in his mind, John fell to sleep, and dreamed a beautiful dream of Sarah running through the meadow singing for all of nature and Gott to hear.

Over the next few days, John waited for an opportune time to broach the subject of his intentions to join the Amish. After working a bit later than usual, John and Jacob finally sat down upon the workbench, and John tried his best to engage Jacob in normal pleasantries. After a short while, John decided to tell Jacob what he wished to do,

"Mr. Williams, sir, I have treasured my time here working with you, and living side by side with your wonderful family. There is something very important that I wish to speak with you about."

"Yes, John, what is this that you need to discuss at this late hour?" replied Jacob.

"I understand that we are both very tired, and the hour is rather late, but this is something that is weighing heavily upon my mind, and something that I must speak with you about, and I prefer that we do so alone," offered John.

"Alright, then. Out with it. What is so important, John?"

"I have given this much thought, and I admire your way of life, and the way that your faith enters into every aspect of life. I have noticed how it makes me feel closer to Gott, and I want to join the faith. I realize that this is a rarity, but it is all that I want. You are an intelligent and observant man, Mr. Williams, and you must have noticed my affection for your lovely Sarah. I know that I cannot ask for her hand unless I am an Amish man. I seek to enter the Amish religion not just for the sake of Sarah, but for my own well-being. I want to fully belong to this community, and I want to worship and live just as you do," said John with as much earnestness as he could muster.

"Mr. Anders, though your intentions seem true and honest to me, you are correct in thinking that an Englischer cannot possibly enter into marriage with my daughter. I will speak to the men of the church before Sunday, but I must warn you that you are about to take on a long and serious obligation to Gott," answered Jacob, much to John's relief. This answer was what he was desperately hoping to hear from Sarah's father. It was proof, however small, that he accepted John as a suitor for Sarah once he converted to the Amish faith. It was something important he would be doing for himself and for Sarah. He had been practicing something special for Jacob, and now seemed the perfect time to say it. John stood up, and without further ado, launched into the Pennsylvania Dutch phrase he had been studying since he arrived. For it was on that very day, that John already knew that he must win the love of Sarah if he was ever to be a happy man,

"Mer sott em sei Eagne net verlosse; Gott verlosst die Seine night," and that is what John said right then and there to Jacob, which translated to "One should not abandon one's own; God does not abandon his own."

Jacob looked like the most surprised man on the face of the earth. Not only had John come to him in the hopes to become Amish, but he had made the effort to speak to him in the Old German. John couldn't have chosen a better phrase for the occasion, and Jacob could not deny John his dreams. Jacob resolved to speak to the other Amish, and begin John's training, "Yes, John. I am very pleased with your dedication to both Gott and my daughter. You shall be worthy of Sarah soon, so you may as well tell her of your intentions, before she sets eyes on another eligible bachelor," he chuckled. John had never seen Jacob smile before, let alone chuckle!

The next day, being Friday morning, John awoke at his normal time with his whole heart bursting with excitement. He wanted very badly to tell Sarah of the conversation that he and her father had had the night before, but he also wanted to choose just the perfect time to tell her. He had it thought out, and he hoped everything went according to plan. He would keep everything a secret from Sarah until tonight.

The day seemed endless to John, as he toiled away at his work. No matter how hot the day became, or how tired he felt, he felt an overwhelming sense of peace come over him, knowing he would eventually become a part of the community he had grown to love in such a short amount of time. Not only had he found a home and a new life filled with hope, he had also found the love of his life, who shared his love of music and singing. It filled him with absolute joy knowing that he was embarking on this new chapter in his life. As the sky darkened with the coming of dusk, John and Jacob stopped work. It was finally time for the family to have supper together. John's most favorite time of the day.

John explained to Jacob that he wanted to wash up and tidy himself before coming into the house for supper, so Jacob certainly sensed what was coming. He was happy for his daughter, but sad to lose her when she eventually married. Hope would have to take over the motherly duties of caring for her boppli bruder, but she had been well trained by her older sister.

Sarah served up the supper, and everyone took their place at the table. Everyone appeared to be hungry, and both her father and John remarked how delicious the chicken pot pie had turned out. She had handpicked the vegetables that she added to the chicken, and she did admit to herself that it tasted quite fresh and hearty. Right on schedule, Jacob excused himself saying that he was worn out. John helped with the cleaning up as he often did, and then Sarah helped put Hope and

Noah to bed, but not without singing a soft and heartwarming bedtime song of "Lavender's Blue." John closed his eyes as he listened to her angel voice. His mother had once sung him the very same lullaby when he was just a small child. It made him feel happy, yet sad that his mother would not get the chance to meet his beloved, or hear her wonderful singing voice.

Sarah emerged from the back bedroom, and joined John by the fire as was their new custom. John said he was feeling very tired, and that it was high time he got to bed, for tomorrow was Saturday, and there was much work to be done on the barn. He asked Sarah to walk with him, and so she did. John and Sarah strolled through the garden pathway towards his shack that had been transformed into a humble home. John said he had heard her singing the delicate lullaby to her sister and brother, and asked her to sing it once again for him as they sat down on the garden bench. Sarah was not surprised at his request, as she knew that John adored her singing. After she had finished the song, John got down upon his knee. Sarah could barely comprehend what was happening, since she was totally unaware of John's important conversation with her daed. John looked into Sarah's big brown eyes, and said what he had been waiting to say to her all night long,

"My dearest Sarah, I have taken the liberty to speak to your father about joining the Amish, and he has agreed that I shall begin my lessons this Sunday service. So, that being settled, I am now worthy of the question I am about to put to you. After my lessons have concluded, and I have become fully Amish, please be my wife. I must have you as my very own, and I shall want to hear you sing to our own future children the special lullaby you have just finished singing to me this night. I love you with all of my heart."

Sarah looked at him, her eyes welling with emotion, as she grabbed hold of his shoulders to hug him snugly in her arms,

"Yes, John, there is nothing in the world that would be more wonderful than becoming your wife! I have felt this since you first surprised me in daed's store."

And so, the two young lovers walked happily to John's little house, dreaming of their future together in the not so distant future...

Ephesians 5:19 "...speaking to one another with psalms, hymns, and songs from the Spirit. Sing and make music from your heart to the Lord..."

HANNAH

<u>December</u>

The service had been lovely as always but Hannah had been unable to concentrate, her mind bustling with dozens of thoughts. As she followed her fiancé's family from the home of one of the member and into the back area of their farm, she wrung her hands nervously.

"Hannah, are you unwell?" She jumped at the sound of Isaac's voice near her ear.

"Not at all! On the contrary, in fact," she replied, peering at him, confusion coloring her face. "What would make you ask such a thing?"

"You seemed not to be paying any attention whatsoever during the sermon. I believe the Bishop scowled at you at one moment." Shocked, Hannah paused in mid step to stare at her husband-to-be, abruptly holding up the line trekking through the field.

"You must be joking!" she cried and then saw the twinkle in Isaac's gentle hazel eyes.

"Perhaps I am but you must admit that your mind has been elsewhere today. What are you thinking about? I noticed the faraway look in your eye from my side of the room!" Hannah laughed and continued toward the barn where the Fisher family had arranged for lunch following their Sunday worship. The winter had been unseasonably warm and Hannah felt somewhat overdressed in her wool cloak. She wished for snow. It did not feel festive without snowflakes gracing the air.

"Well? What is it that plagues your thoughts? Are you reconsidering our marriage?" Again, Isaac's warm eyes lit up with laughter and Hannah grinned broadly at his jesting.

"Certainly not! I am simply concerned about Christmas," Hannah replied, her thoughts beginning to race once more. It was Isaac's turn to show confusion.

"What of Christmas? It is the loveliest time of year. Surely you can't be glum!"

"Not in the least," Hannah replied as they made their way into the spacious structure to join the rest of the congregation. "I am simply worried I have not prepared properly. I have made presents of all of the children and for my parents but I feel as though I have forgotten someone. Which brings me to the Christmas cards. I am always concerned that I have left out a family. Can you imagine how much embarrassment that would bring to us should I omit a single family? What's more is I set up the nativity scene in the front of our home and I cannot find one wise man and two angels. Now I suspect that Rachel has been playing with them but I have yet to find them and she denies knowing their whereabouts. I must have father whittle some for me or else it will be a disaster!"

Suddenly Hannah felt as though a huge weight had been lifted off her shoulders with the confession. Isaac burst into laughter.

"Oh, Hannah! The things which make you fret do amuse me endlessly. It is Christmastime, *liebchen*. It is not a time of worry and fret. That is for the English. We are only to give thanks and spend time with those dearest to us."

"I know, Isaac, but I cannot help wanting Christmas to be perfect! It is my favorite time of the year. And look! This year we haven't even any snow! It hardly seems proper to even set up a tree without the candlelight twinkling off the snow." Hannah pouted but immediately smiled as the truth of his words struck her. Of course he was right; this was not a time of stress. Their way was that of peace and order, not to be overshadowed by the trivialities which the outside word concerned themselves. It was what made the Amish community so special; the ability to block out the unnecessary and focus on the beauty of the basics in life. Hannah could not be happier. She and Isaac had become betrothed in February and their impending marriage was announced to the community in October as per tradition. They had plans to wed the following winter as per tradition and she could not have hoped for a better mate. Despite their engagement, Isaac continued to act as though they were newly enamored with one another, bequeathing her with beautiful flowers and penning poetry for her, words which made her warm to her soul. She was excited to begin her life with him. It seemed that the wedding was millennia away, not merely a year.

"Ah, Hannah, you may worry but your Christmas spirit is infectious," Bishop Philips told her, overhearing the last of their conversation. Blushing scarlet, Hannah turned to acknowledge him, bowing her head.

"Your sermon was well received today, Bishop," Hannah told him, trying to recover from her embarrassment. "It is a rare treat to hear you speak lately. I'm afraid we miss hearing your voice in service. I am pleasantly surprised you have joined us today."

"Unfortunately, I have had business in other districts as of late but I am happy to be back at home. I haven't had the opportunity to congratulate on your betrothal. Isaac, you have done well for yourself. The Yoder family is well respected in our district. Perhaps you will bless them with a son." The Bishop smiled at the couple.

"Not that the Yoder women are any less hard working than any of the men in our community. How is your family? I do not see your father here today," the Bishop continued, looking about, a sudden cloud covering his brown eyes. Hannah and Isaac followed his gaze. Hannah's mother, Ruth stood speaking with several other women while her sisters, Rachel and Miriam ran through the barn, playing a game of tag with some of the other children. As the three continued to look about, Hannah felt a stab of panic in her stomach. It was unheard of for her father, Mark to be absent from church services. She had spent the previous week in Isaac's district at a family member's home. Hannah had been slowly learning the workings of his father's farm at the insistence of Mark who thought it best she understood the complexities of her husband's land as much as possible. As Hannah's cousins resided in close proximity to Isaac's farm, the transition had been seamless and it allowed for their sweet courtship to continue uninterrupted. This also meant, however, that Hannah was not as informed as to the comings and goings of her own family. Brow furrowed, Hannah excused herself and hurried over to her mother, despite Isaac's reactionary hand on her arm to stop her.

"*Mamm*, where is *Daed*?" she whispered in her mother's ear urgently without preamble. Ruth gave Hannah a reproving look and politely exited the conversation in which she was involved.

"Mind your manners, Hannah!" Ruth Yoder chided her daughter.

"I'm sorry Mammi, I am just worried about him. It is unlike him to miss service. I can't recall one instance prior to this one in fact!" Hannah insisted. Seeing her oldest daughter's distress, Ruth's face softened.

"Your father was away at market in Pittsburgh over the weekend. He was expecting to be back last night but the weather turned so he must have been detained. He will likely be home when we return." Hannah exhaled with relief and returned to her fiancé and the Bishop where she reiterated what she had been told. A bell rang to indicate that the meal was about to be served and they all sat at the long tables set up in the middle of building. Yet as they bowed their heads and grace was said, once again, Hannah felt herself distracted by unstoppable thoughts. This time, however, they were not of snowfalls and wise men. Suddenly she her mind was focussed completely on the whereabouts of her father.

"I don't mind, Hannah but I cannot help but feel you are overreacting somewhat," Isaac informed her as they pulled their carriage toward the Yoder farm.

"He is my father. I must know that he is well, Isaac," Hannah replied.

"*Liebchen*, he has been going to market since well before you were born. I am sure he is well. You will see." Isaac smiled boyishly at her and encouraged the horses onward. Hannah felt an uncharacteristic smidgen of annoyance at his placation. She gave him a sidelong look but said nothing. She hoped he was right but some inherent sense told her something was amiss. Inclement weather or not, Mark Yoder would have been at worship. His devotion to God was his priority, probably above his own health and safety. Hannah knew her father. He would have risked riding in a blizzard to honor his commitment to the community. Her mother had arrived back from the Miller farm with Rachel and Miriam and the pale afternoon light was already becoming dark, forsaking dusk altogether.

"I do not see his wagon," Hannah mumbled as they pulled to a stop. Alarm growing in her chest, Hannah recognized the Bishop's carriage which was parked behind the modest house. Hannah did not wait for Isaac to escort her from her seat and instead was running up the front steps to toward the door. As she flew inside the house, she stopped in her tracks. Her mother was on her knees, surrounded by Rachel and Miriam, a look of shock upon their faces. Tears had slipped from their cheeks to the wood floor. Bishop Phillips stood, solemn faced at the base of the stairs, his hat in his hands, his lips pursed into a fine line. They did not need to speak. Hannah already knew.

<u>January</u>

"Hannah, Isaac came calling again," Miriam told her, pushing open the door to the bedroom where her sister sat brushing her long hair, placing it into sections for braiding. Hannah did not respond. Instead she continued to count the strokes, slowly, meticulously smoothing down the strands.

"Hannah? Hannah!" Miriam strode into the room and snatched the utensil from her sister's grip. The older girl looked up in surprise and instinctively grabbed it back.

"What is it?" she demanded, rising to her feet menacingly.

"Isaac was here," Miriam said again. "He would like you to contact him when you are well."

"I am well, thank you. I am simply busy. With *Daed* in the hospital, fighting for his life, someone needs to help *Mamm* run the farm, Miriam. I cannot up and run off to help him when Isaac has able bodied brothers there. What does he want from me?" Her words were like a torrent of venom and twelve-year-old Miriam stepped back, shocked at her tone.

"I believe that he wants to know if you're well, Hannah. I don't think he wants you to help him on the farm," she offered, timidly, tears filling her eyes. Hannah was immediately contrite but her anger would not lessen.

"Thank you, Miriam. I will be in contact with Isaac shortly." Her sister immediately retreated from the bedroom, closing the door in her wake but Hannah heard her sister's stifled sob before she retreated down the stairs. Hannah knew that her tone had been unreasonably harsh but she could not seem to alleviate the insurmountable rage which had filled her since the horrendous accident her father had endured a mere month before. The driver who had injured Mark so severely on that lone road heading home from the city had yet to be caught and Hannah knew she would not rest until the person had been apprehended and brought to justice. Christmas had come and gone in an unmemorable blur, still filled with family and friends but in a much more somber tone than the joy of the season typically brought. The family had left the candles lit in the windows well after other members of the community had extinguished theirs, a constant flame for others to keep Mark in their prayers. Hannah remembered thinking that the nativity scene was ruined and she had reprimanded Rachel harshly for playing with the wooden characters, reducing the child to a blubbering mess. Much more than that, Hannah could not recall about holiday. There had been an exchange of gifts but Mark's had lay unopened at the hearth and Hannah did not have any recollection of what she had received. Hannah's mother had continued her duty, tending to the farm and caring for the children and Hannah had stepped in to assist as opposed to joining Isaac. At first, Isaac had attempted to stay nearby, offering his unselfish aide to the Yoder family but eventually Hannah's increasingly sullen behavior had driven him home to his family's land. Still, he had frequently visited his beloved to see how she was faring. More often than not, Hannah made herself unavailable for reasons no one could comprehend. While she never admitted it to anyone, she blamed Isaac also for her father's fate. *If only he had been more vigilante, heeded my words more carefully when I suggested that something was amiss with father,* she told herself time and again. It did not matter that Mark Yoder had been hit on the Saturday night, well before Hannah had any inkling that there was trouble. In Hannah's grief she was beyond reason and all she had remaining was her intense anger. It was irrelevant whom was the recipient of her rage. It needed to be released and Hannah ensured that it was so. Mark's initial prognosis had been grim. The internal damage to his organs was severe and he had several broken bones. He was still on a life support machine in the hospital where he had been taken following being struck. Hannah could not bear to see her strong, vital father in such a condition and had refused to attend his side despite her mother's pleading.

"Hannah, your father needs you there," Ruth had begged her daughter. "Please swallow your repulsion and spend some time at his side. He can hear your prayers."

"He can hear my prayers from here, Mamm. It makes not difference if I am here or there. I cannot bear to see him in such a state with wires poking out of him. Hospitals are filled with harsh lights and harsher people," Hannah countered. "I will not be any good to him there. He knows I am with him in spirit."

Any amount of argument had been futile and eventually Ruth gave up, attending the county hospital with only her two youngest.

"God will not allow him to be taken from us," Ruth assured Hannah one night, attempting to connect with her distraught oldest child.

"God should not have allowed him to have been struck in the first place!" Hannah had yelled back. "God should have been watching out for him. God should have rendered the driver comatose and on life support!"

There was no point in debating the issue. In her mind, Hannah would not rest until she saw the face of the person responsible for the atrocity writhing in shame, guilt and agony.

<u>February</u>

"Ma'am I understand your anger but there we are doing everything we can."

Hannah's blue eyes flashed but she checked her temper.

"Sir, it has been almost three months and you have absolutely no leads regarding the driver of the vehicle which struck my father. Surely you should be exploring other avenues to catch this animal! Doesn't it concern you that this kind of person is driving on your streets where your children walk?"

"Hannah!" Isaac gently placed his hand on her shoulder as she rose from her chair to confront the police detective at the desk. He turned apologetically to the detective.

"Hannah has been under a lot of stress since the accident," Isaac told the man who nodded understandingly.

"Of course, we fully get that and we sympathize," Detective Adams replied. "I have heard that your father is no longer on life support. We are all very happy to hear that."

Hannah felt her hands clench into fists, her nails digging into her palms.

"Yes, praise the Lord for small favors," she answered shortly, her eyes narrowing, ignoring Isaac's fingers which were now increasing pressure on her shoulder. "However, that does not change anything. Is this why nothing has been done to find the monster responsible? Because he is alive? Next time he may not be so lucky if this person is still on the road!"

"Miss Yoder, I assure you that we are doing everything we can but it is very difficult with the circumstances. There were no witnesses, it was a dark road..."

Hannah threw up her hands. She understood. Mark Yoder was not a priority to these people. He would have to be dead or English for them to care. They were just going to say words until she left them alone. Worried she would not be able to contain a barrage of words threatening to escape her lips, she turned to leave without responding. Hannah heard Isaac apologizing for her rudeness once more but Hannah did not wait for her fiancé. Moments later, he was at her side, breathing heavily from chasing her down the crowded street. Under normal circumstances, Hannah would have been unnerved by the throng of people in her midst. It was not like her to visit town, much preferring the quiet way of her community but it had been months and there had been no advancement regarding the driver who had struck her father. Against her mother's pleas, Hannah had taken it upon herself to meet with the detective face-to-face.

"Please, Hannah, Bishop Phillips has been in constant contact with the police. You must not go and bother them."

"If not me, then who?" Hannah had demanded.

"Go see your father! He needs you!" Ruth implored. But the words had fallen upon deaf ears and Ruth had summoned Isaac to accompany her now wayward daughter into town. Isaac had appeared as Hannah was setting off.

"Hannah! That was rude!" He breathed, struggling to keep up with her brisk stride.

"Well perhaps that's what they need, rudeness. Niceties don't seem to be getting us anywhere."

"Hannah, I'm sure they are doing everything they can – "

"It is not enough!" Hannah snapped. Isaac stopped walking, taken aback by her tone. Hannah had never had occasion to speak to him in such a manner. He watched after the woman he was destined to marry and he wondered what had happened to the gentle, even tempered girl he had courted. He understood she was frazzled, not acting rationally but deep down, he hoped that girl was not lost forever.

<u>March</u>

"Hannah, you have not been at worship in several weeks."

The statement was blunt but not filled with accusation. Bishop Phillips simply stared at her, his brown eyes wise with understanding. She shrugged nonchalantly and did not turn from the hens from which she was collecting eggs.

"God knows where I am," she responded flippantly. Bishop Phillips drew closer to her inside the coop, ignoring the squawking of the animals in his midst.

"It is not simply of God knowing where to find you," he told her, gently. "Worship is a place of community, a place where others can shoulder your burden while asking for the Lord's help."

Hannah reeled around to glare at him.

"What does the community know of shouldering my burden?" she asked. "Can they find the animal who ran down my father like a rabid dog in the street? Have they made him pay penance for the harm he has caused my family?"

A warm, fatherly hand reached her shoulder and the Bishop smiled weakly.

"Perhaps not, child, but your suffering is our suffering also. We grow together and we will support one another. That is what makes us strong. You cannot fight this burden alone."

"I am not alone," Hannah retorted. "I have my family. I have Isaac."

But even as she said the words, Hannah tried to remember the last time she had spent more than a few moments with her betrothed. She could not. She shoved the thought from her mind. It did not matter. The only importance was figuring out who had hurt her father. Isaac would have to understand that her priority was with her father.

<u>April</u>

"Hannah! Hannah!"

Miriam and Rachel's footsteps could be heard reverberating through her bedroom well before the door flew open and the twins appeared. Her heart in her throat, Hannah turned away from the window out of which she had been staring for well over an hour, lost in thought.

"What is it? Is it *Daed*? Is he dead?"

Shocked, the girls recoiled at her words, smiles fading from their lips.

"No!" Rachel cried. "Of course not! Why would you say such a thing?"

In truth, Hannah had been waiting for news of the like and had been since the day he had been hospitalized. Her heart began to slow and she forced herself to smile at her sisters.

"I'm sorry. What is it?"

"He's awake! *Daed* is awake!"

Hannah's slowing pulse picked up speed once more. She flung herself into her siblings' arms and the three rejoiced at the news.

"He is? When did this happen? What did the doctors say?" Hannah whipped the questions at them rapid fire. Ruth appeared in the doorway. Her face was gaunt from exhaustion and emotion.

"He will still need some time to recover in the hospital," Ruth answered. "But his ribs are healing as well as his kidneys." Hannah pulled away from the twins and looked at her mother, her face alight with excitement. *Now we will catch you! Daed will identify the driver and it will all be over!*

"Did he say anything?" she pressed. "Can he identify the driver? Or the vehicle? Does he know who hit him?"

Ruth's sky colored eyes clouded over and she regarded her daughter for a moment.

"Hannah, it is not healthy for you to focus so direly on the driver. God will sort out what to do with him. You must instead think of your father and concentrate on good thoughts." Hannah scowled at her mother.

"I am focussed on *Daed*! That is why I want to find out who did this to him! Why am I met with resistance at every turn? You, Isaac, Bishop Phillips. Am I the only one who cares about seeing justice served?"

Ruth pursed her lips together and did not reply. Hannah continued to stare at her mother.

"Well? What did he say? Did he identify the man or not?" she demanded. Ruth sighed heavily.

"No, Hannah. He cannot speak. He had a stroke."

<u>May</u>

Springtime held the promise of new birth for everyone in the community but Hannah. She found herself tending to chores indoor more and more. Isaac had ceased visiting altogether and Hannah found herself in the police station once a week, hounding Detective Adams mercilessly. Where the women in the community would have typically begun to make suggestions for her wedding, offering assistance and chattering cheerfully of their own nuptials, Hannah found herself almost isolated, something she was quite content in discovering. The feeling of helplessness which had overwhelmed her was becoming a suffocating blanket as more time passed and left her no closer to finding the heathen who had hurt her father. She still had not gone to the hospital to see Mark, despite reports from her family that he was faring quite well. He still had not managed to recoup his motor skills and Hannah did not want the face of a crippled man plaguing her already dark thoughts. She would not rest until someone had paid.

<u>June</u>

"You are attending service."

Her voice was flat and left no room for argument. Hannah opened her mouth to speak but caught the anger in her mother's usually gentle eyes and thought better of voicing her thoughts. Grudgingly, she retreated to her room to ready herself for worship.

The family hosting church services was a neighbor and the Yoder family arrived just as Bishop Phillips rose to speak. He fixated his eyes upon Hannah and began to preach of forgiveness. Hannah closed her ears and averted her eyes. *I will forgive when the driver asks for forgiveness. Not one moment before. And even then, I may not.*

July

He came home on a Tuesday and several members of the community were present to welcome Mark. They brought flowers and honey and bombarded him and the family with well wishes. Isaac and his family had driven in also but Hannah only watched the event from her bedroom window, unable to watch her enfeebled father slowly stumble his way up the steps of the veranda. Her eyes filled with tears but whether they were of guilt or pain, she was not sure. As Mark made his way inside with the help of his wife and two youngest daughters, Isaac lifted his eyes toward Hannah's bedroom window. His own eyes were filled with sadness and Hannah quickly ducked back behind the curtains, not willing to look at him. It had been a long while since they had spent time together and she admitted that she missed his company dearly. She often wondered what he was doing and if he thought of her. The look on his face told Hannah that he did long for her as she did him. Swallowing the urge to run downstairs and beg him for forgiveness, Hannah sat on the edge of the bed. She wondered if anything would ever be the same again.

August

"Hannah! Hannah!"

Rachel almost knocked Hannah over as she barreled into the barn. Hannah looked up at her quickly.

"What is it?"

"*Daed* said his first clear word!" Hannah felt hope swell in her chest.

"What did he say?" she asked, wiping her hands on her apron and following Rachel out of the building, toward the house.

"He said 'Hannah.' He's asking for you!"

<u>September</u>

Progress was swift from that moment onward. Every day, Mark Yoder began to say more. He was required to see a specialist in town to assist him in his walking but Hannah was beginning to see signs of the same, strapping man she had admired her whole life. She found it less painful to be in his presence but she still could not help but feel enraged at his condition. When Hannah did stay at his side, she pressed him for details of the accident. To her relief, he recalled a great deal and Hannah feverishly wrote down the details as Mark remembered, every day adding more to the description. Finally, after three weeks, she had a proper sketch of the vehicle and possibly the driver which she immediately took to the police station. *Now we've got you!* She thought smugly.

<u>October</u>

"Are we still to marry?"

The question startled Hannah as she had not heard Isaac at her back. He had been watching her from the porch as she hummed to herself, picking wildflowers. Oddly, the upcoming wedding had been fresh in her mind for the first time in months. Since delivering the description to the police, Hannah had felt as though they were nearing absolution and a giant weight seemed to have been lifted from her shoulders. She stared in surprise at her fiancé.

"I certainly hope so, Isaac. Are you reconsidering?" She felt faint as she waited for him to answer. Slowly, Isaac made his way down the steps and toward his betrothed.

"I feel as though we have become very distant these past months, Hannah. I wondered if you still wished for us to marry." She met the distance between them and offered him her hands.

"Forgive me, Isaac! I have been consumed with worry for my father. Of course I have never thought for a moment that you and I would not be wed." Isaac eagerly accepted her hands and squeezed them gently, smiling with relief.

"I am glad you have finally decided to forgive and move on," he told her. "I knew the sensible woman I know was in there somewhere."

Hannah beamed back at him.

"It will be very easy to move on once this man is caught! I believe the police will finally catch him now!"

The smile died on Isaac's lips as he stared at Hannah. He realized that she was still consumed with the idea of catching the driver. Wisely, he said nothing but a sense of unease filled his stomach. Would this never end?

<u>November</u>

"You must be very excited with the upcoming wedding, Hannah. It has been quite a year for you and your family. It will be a relief to have cause for celebration over bad times, I would say," Bishop Phillips said after service. Hannah smiled widely and nodded, glancing at Isaac. He smiled meekly.

"Yes, we are looking forward to it. A Christmas wedding may seem a bit ostentatious but it is my favorite time of year and Isaac has been kind enough to indulge my whimsy on this matter," Hannah answered happily.

"Well I think it is a wonderful idea. It will only solidify your union with Christ. I am happy to see your father up and about."

"Yes, he is already back into manning the farm as he was prior to the accident."

"Well that is wonderful news, Hannah. It must certainly alleviate your desire to see the perpetrator arrested. It was not good for you to be so fixated on such negative thoughts for so long," the Bishop told her, turning to nod at other members of the congregation.

"No, Bishop, I can focus on other things now. The police are closing in on the animal now that my father has given them somewhere to look. We will have our justice in due time. I must leave it in their hands now." The Bishop looked at Hannah sharply.

"Your father knows who hit him?"

"He gave a very accurate description of the man, yes," Hannah replied. "But as you say, Bishop, it is in God's hands now. I have decided to focus more on my husband-to-be and deal with the criminal when he is found."

Bishop Phillips nodded, his eyes dark.

"Yes, it is in God's hands," he agreed.

December

The police were standing on her porch and Hannah felt her heart leap into her throat.

"Miss Yoder? Is your father home?" the detective asked her, peering over her shoulder. She nodded eagerly and granted them entry. Mark sat in a rocking chair in the front room. He rose to his feet with an agility he did not possess even two weeks prior.

"Please do come in, officers," he told them, cordially. Awkwardly, the detectives ventured into the humble home and stood in the doorway.

"Have you found the man responsible?" Hannah demanded. "Is that why you're here?"

Mark gave her a reproachful look.

"Hannah, where are your manners? Would you like a beverage?" Both men shook their heads and fidgeted nervously.

"Well?" Hannah demanded when there was silence. "Have you news?"

"Hannah!" Mark chided again but the lead detective held up his hand and nodded.

"Yes, Miss Yoder. We have your man. Someone has turned himself in."

Hannah's face went through a variety of changes; hope, shock and then anger.

"He turned himself in?" she almost yelled. "After one year? What kind of monster lets a family suffer for an entire year before confessing his crime?"

"Hannah…"

"Yes, Miss Yoder but frankly, in these situations, it is extremely difficult to find hit and run drivers. We are very lucky that someone did come forward at all," the policeman interjected. "But I do understand your frustration."

"I doubt it," Hannah mumbled. "Where is he?"

"He is in the county lock up. We would like your father to come with us to see if he can be identified in a line up but he had fully confessed to the accident."

"Who is he? A young, drunk English boy?" Hannah asked contemptuously, already envisioning the short haired punk, smoking a marijuana cigarette. Again, an uncomfortable silence ensued. Hannah stared at the men expectantly.

"Who is he?"

Detective Adams cleared his throat.

"It is someone you know," he said evasively. Hannah exchanged concerned looks with her father.

"Who?" she pressed.

"He is your Bishop. Daniel Phillips."

"Hello Hannah."

Hannah felt her legs turn to jelly as she stared at her much-loved Bishop behind the bars of the county jail.

"It is true," she whispered. "How did this happen?"

"I wish I could explain it to you, child but there is nothing I can say which will take away what you and your family have endured over this year."

"Please tell me what happened," she begged, her eyes filled with tears. The Bishop took a breath and told her the story he had relived in his head over and over since the day it had happened.

He had travelled the road hundreds, if not thousands of times before but Bishop Phillips had not slept more than two hours a night in over three weeks. There had been minor unrest in two of the neighboring districts, some petty squabbling which should have resolved itself but somehow a miniscule issue had become a weeks long debate. He was grateful that he was finally able to return home to his district. The car in which he rode had been a gift from a Bishop in one of the districts who had taken pity upon his constant state of commute. Bishop Phillips had to admit that it was more luxurious than his hard riding horse and cart but he also knew that he should not get too attached.

As the headlights lit the way around the road, his heart leapt into his throat. A doe stood frozen in the road, shocked by the onset. In his exhaustion, it took a few seconds for his reaction time to match up with his vision. He slammed on the brakes and veered to the left of the road, barely grazing the tail of the animal but full on impacting something else; a horse drawn cart. The mare whinnied in pain and shock as the Bishop struggled to steady the still moving vehicle. As all was still, Bishop Phillips opened the door to the car and ran toward the now toppled buggy. Inside lay the still body of Mark Yoder, seemingly lifeless. Bishop Phillips stood stock still, unsure of what to do. I must stay and wait for help, he told himself. Then he remembered the two glasses of wine he had consumed with supper. Slowly, he backed up and slipped back into the car, driving away undetected into the black night.

Tears fell from her lids onto her cheeks as she looked at the broken man before her. She thought of how badly she had wanted him to suffer but all she could think of was how much he had already suffered. He must have wanted to ease her agony a thousand times but had been trapped in his own nightmare.

"I understand that you must loathe me, Hannah. You have every right to feel as such," Bishop Phillips told her, his voice cracking. Gently, Hannah reached between the bars and offered the Bishop her hands. He grabbed them instantly and looked at her pleadingly.

"I forgive you," she said simply.

<u>Christmas</u>

"Oh, Hannah you look beautiful," Ruth told her daughter, embracing her warmly. "I have been looking forward to this for so long!"

Hannah laughed.

"Yes, me too Mammi," she joked and lovingly returned her mother's caress. She looked at herself in the mirror one last time. She vowed to her reflection that with this new start she would forsake all anger and rely on God to give her strength in the worst of times. She knew how fortunate she was that Isaac had been strong enough to stand by her during such a trying time and she would never forget it. She turned and looked at her mother and sisters.

"Are you ready?" Miriam asked, hopping back and forth from one foot to another. Hannah looked around and suddenly her stomach dropped.

"Where is *Daed*?" she asked, feeling a familiar sense of panic seize her. The curtain was quickly drawn and Mark strolled in, his gait strong and perfect.

"I am here, *liebchen*. Do you think I would miss giving away my oldest daughter?" he answered. His voice was slightly slower than it had been but his words were perfectly pronounced. There was no sign of the stroke he had suffered. Hannah exhaled. Everything was right again.